GW00384997

DYKEVERSIONS

DYKEVERSIONS

Lesbian Short Fiction

Edited by
The Lesbian Writing
and Publishing Collective

The
Women's
·Press·

CANADIAN CATALOGUING IN PUBLICATION DATA

Dykeversions: lesbian short fiction

ISBN 0-88961-110-6

1. Short stories, Canadian (English) – Women authors.*
2. Short stories, Canadian (English) – 20th century.*
3. Lesbianism – Fiction. I. Lesbian Writing and Publishing Collective.

PS8323.L47D94 1986   C813'.54'08 C86-09 4947-8
PR9197.32D94   1986

Cover art by Beatrice Baily
This book was produced by the collective effort
of the members of the Women's Press
Printed and bound in Canada

Published by the Women's Press
229 College Street No. 204
Toronto, Ontario M5T 1R4

CONTENTS

Introduction 7

Notes About Racism in the Process 11

CLUSTERS *Oriental-Asian Coyote* 17

LACEY LOVE LETTERS *Diana Meredith* 20

APRONS AND HOMEMADE BREAD *Candis J. Graham* 25

THE HAUNTING OF BLUE LAKE *Nora D. Randall* 32

JUST ANOTHER DAY *Anne Cameron* 41

ONE BECAME A ROOFER *Marlene Wildeman* 51

KEYNOTES *Michele Paulse* 65

THE REPORT CARD *Carol Allen* 70

A FIGURE OF SPEECH *Mary Louise Adams* 73

AN UNPOSTED LETTER, APRIL 15, 1985
Jennifer Lee Martin 80

ONE IS TWO IS TWO IS ONE *Kate Lazier* 84

SUBROUTINE *Judith Quinlan* 97

SUBSURFACE SONICS *Suniti Namjoshi* 108

DINING OUT WITH CHARLES *Janine Fuller* 109

THE BALLAD OF THE DEEP BLUE SEA *Jean Roberta* 116

ASTA'S HERE ... *Sarah Sheard* 127

POLISHED & PERFECT *Ingrid MacDonald* 130

TURNING THIRTY-ONE *Heather Ramsay* 147

"I ASKED ABOUT US" *Daphne Marlatt* 159

CHEMO DREAMS *J.A. Hamilton* 161

THE KIDNAPPING *Naomi Binder Wall* 164

OUT OF HER SKIN, OUT OF HER VOICE *Nila Gupta* 168

Contributors' Notes 179

INTRODUCTION

AS LESBIANS, there is a certain outrageousness to all our lives which are diversions from the expected path of womanly life. But we also don't live in the world pared down to our sexual identity. We are women layered with various identities; we are mothers (and not), women with material privileges (and not), women of colour (and not), bikers (and not), carpenters (and not), computer hacks (and not), young (and not). Hence the various versions of being a dyke.

An anthology is the perfect vehicle for imagining such diversity. *Dykeversions: Lesbian Short Fiction* is the first completed project of the Lesbian Writing and Publishing Collective which was founded in 1984 to assist the publishing of writing by and about lesbians. We decided on an anthology of short fiction for our first publication because it would enable us to represent a number of different writers, because we knew of no such anthology in process in Canada, and because we thought it would encourage lesbian writers to do yet more writing. We received over eighty pieces, suggesting that many lesbians *are* writing. But the difficulty of getting material published discourages emerging writers. Even women we knew required personal encouragement (even badgering) before they'd send us their writing. So here's the first of a series which we hope will encourage lesbian writing.

What *exactly* were we looking for? As lesbians, breaking forms in standard definitions of women, we hoped that this collection would break some form in standard literary definitions. In our letters and advertisements, we asked for "fictions" because we were hoping to receive some works that were not quite standard poetry, but not quite standard prose either. We did receive a few, and these are included.

It is hard to make any generalizations about why a piece of fiction worked for one of us and not another, harder still to account for those stories that all of us agreed on. We had intense disagreements too, and when those occurred, we went with the majority, agreed to disagree, or published a story because it gave voice to things generally not spoken about. We also decided to exclude previously published material and to publish only one piece per author so as to give previously unheard voices a chance.

The process of putting together an anthology was not, in the end, however, a simple matter of picking stories we liked. It was also a political process which as feminists is part of our living and developing. We are, at present, a diverse lesbian editorial collective and our differences initiated much theoretical discussion as well as the practical discussions of the stories at hand. We are: women of colour, white women, middle-class and working class women; feminists, socialist feminists, anarcha-feminists and First World (misknown as Third World) Feminists. Still, our networks were not as extensive and diverse as they could be. Consequently, most of the writers are white and from large cities. We didn't receive any writing from disabled women, Native women, women from the Maritimes, or women from the Territories.

We also hoped that these fictions, while making lesbians visible, would break the stereotype that lesbians can be defined or categorized as having any particular qualities or attributes beyond that of our sexuality. Beyond that we assumed no simple commonality, no single vantage point by which lesbians see the world and certainly no single image we wished to project. We did not feel that only the most acceptable face of our lives should be put forward. There are themes of violence as well as domestic bliss. There are raunchy, erotic stories as well as stories in which never a kiss passes their lips, work that is outrageous, some that is sedate.

We hope you enjoy *Dykeversions*.

> *Maureen FitzGerald, Nila Gupta, Michele Paulse,*
> *Ellen Quigley, and Heather Ramsay.*

NOTES ABOUT RACISM
IN THE PROCESS

SINCE DISCUSSIONS of racism played a large part in our collective process, we felt a responsibility to present some of this discussion to the public.

LESBIANS OF COLOUR CAUCUS STATEMENT

Our constant struggle as women of colour on this collective has been around racism. There were times when we were on the brink of leaving and withdrawing stories we had solicited or written, and letting the anthology be what it would have been without our energy – a white women's anthology that included racist content. This was one of the ways in which having a lesbians of colour caucus during and after meetings was supportive and strengthening.

White women did nothing at the beginning nor during the process of the anthology to educate themselves on how their white privilege, and their actions and lack of actions as white women are racist. Because they did not take any reponsibility for anti-racism education themselves, we were put in the unwilling position of educating them when we recognized racism and they did not. This made our process in the collective very time consuming and frustrating.

There were several ways in which white privilege was manifested on the collective. Again, women of colour were asked to join an all-white collective at virtually the last minute. We walked in at the point when the form of the book had been decided and the networking phase was assumed to be complete. The invitation to join clearly represented a token effort to include lesbians of colour, for we heard of no other lesbians of colour, individuals or groups, being asked to join the collective. Tokenism is racism.

The networking phase of the project again demonstrated tokenism. When we walked into the Lesbian Writing and Publishing Collective, we realized networking had not been done in the women of colour communities, though extensive networking had been done through the so-called feminist network. White women asking their few lesbian of colour friends and acquaintances or calling on the same high-profile writers of colour again and again does not in any way constitute networking.

White women must question why it is that they must go out of their network in order to reach women of colour. Does this not say something about their established network? The feminist network in Canada is a white feminist network, and exclusive networking such as this reproduces racism. It ensures that only the voices of white women are called upon, encouraged and heard. Publishing any anthology that says nothing about *our* lives, *our* struggles, or *our* joys is racism by exclusion.

White women on the collective clearly did not know where to do this networking, nor did they make it a priority to learn how to network amongst all women. The message was clear: If we were concerned about our voices being excluded, then we should do something about it.

During the process of reading, discussing and choosing stories, we often felt like we were guards of the anthology — guarding against the inclusion of stories with racist content. We argued against simply editing racist stories. Since we had no reassurance that a writer's racist writing would not continue, we did not want them to look good. It is unsettling to think that if we had not been here to make the white women aware of racism in several submissions, those stories may well have been published.

At the time we came on the collective the submissions were, with one exception, all from white lesbian writers and several of these were racist. This raised several questions for us: had we been invited merely to perform the role of guards – to "fix" the anthology at the last minute, make it more representative, and make it free from racism? Why had there been no energy put into networking amongst women of colour? We did not want to put energy into looking at racist stories; we wanted to put energy into stories which told the truth about our lives, from our perspective. By leaving it to us to do most of the work, white women were saying that racism is not a white women's issue and networking amongst women of colour is not the responsibility of white women.

From the time we joined the collective we confronted the white women about their white privilege and racism. We hope they will do things differently next time.

We decided to stay in the collective because of our commitment to lesbian of colour writing. Writing is a powerful medium. We wanted to ensure that the power of the voices and visions of lesbians of colour erupt through the racist fabric of feminist publishing.

Michele and Nila

WHITE LESBIANS' STATEMENT

Some lesbians of colour took the risk of joining this previously all-white group. They put the issue of racism on the collective agenda. This brought forth a number of previously undiscussed problems in how we as white women were operating within a collective. It should not have been the singular responsibility of women of colour to raise the issue of racism; that they had to is part of the racism that we white women have to recognize and confront. Even in using the term "we white women," we are acutely aware of how unfamiliar those words are. We are used to saying "women" or "lesbians," when what we really mean is "we white women" and "we white lesbians." This is the racism of exclusion that we must challenge.

We assumed that the participation of women of colour would automatically enlarge our networking process. This laid responsibility on their shoulders alone for contacting women of colour. In this, we made the mistake of putting the end-product before the process. The anthology was underway, letters and advertisements were sent out for submissions, networks were established, and deadlines set because we wanted the anthology out within a year (an unrealistic expectation at that point anyway). None of us had the clarity and courage to stop the process and say, "There's something wrong here – we have to start over."

What have we learned from this discussion of racism in our process? Racism is not only the direct expression of hatred; racism also lies in the complicit acceptance of the status quo – the acceptance of structures as they exist. Our network, our actions and our failures to act create and enforce the invisibility of lesbians who are not white. Racism by exclusion has the power to perpetuate racist structures. We have to confront *all* our assumptions, shake them up, air them, not only in relation to the process of assessing stories, but also, and more importantly, in relation to the process of constructing our group, connecting with other women writing, and interacting with one another in the group.

As white members of a group that has a women of colour caucus, we need to educate ourselves to the ways that our racism works and to be open to the experience that the women of colour are willing to share with us, without expecting them to take full responsibility for educating us about racism.

In developing a network of writers we need to put more effort toward soliciting materials from those lesbians who have not previously submitted material. It is not enough to send equal encouragement to all groups. Women who feel invisible are not as likely to send material as those who already have a strong presence. As lesbians we are invisible to begin with; racism adds to that invisibility. If we look at a structure of oppression that oppresses by gender, sexual orientation, race, class, language and religion, we may begin to understand how difficult it is to make a commitment to lesbians of other races that is strong enough to encourage and convince them to submit material to us. We have to make more effort if we, as white women, are ever to make those links.

For the two of us, this education and this effort is an ongoing process that has only begun to take shape.

Ellen and Maureen

CLUSTERS

Oriental-Asian Coyote

I AM MORE AGGRESSIVE than I look.

I wish I could write an erotic short story like Lee Lynch's *French Mercedes* fantasy, which would make you smile and find so interesting, that you'd hate to put it down.

> I had a lesbian dream on Sunday morning.
> Something to do with a Japanese doll
> sliding   •
> dashing
> after a scared girl in a kimono.
> It could have been a repeated dream
> because I felt I had seen it before.
>
> I also remembered feeling
> I was in Michigan half-heartedly
> regretting that two younger
> Japanese girls there were straight.
>
> I learnt at Michigan that
> we as Oriental have never

been accepted by other womyn
as white
nor are we thought of as colour womyn.

Asian womyn in part or whole – It isn't just me who always feels invisible.

What would you do if you were invited to a private party? You know a member of this group casually. You feel out of yourself when you walk into the house – into a strange room filled with womyn you don't know, had only seen at other parties or at a womyn's parade.

You feel so uncomfortable. All their eyes on you.

What do they see?
Oriental-Asian dyke who looks
too young to drink?
Or the image of myself?
A small but tough and proud
Asian womyn.

I am more aggressive than I look.

I love to look baby-butchy because I will never pass as a bull-dyke.

I have someone I consider my role model. She is a lesbian of colour. Sweet, smart, strong, sexy, gentle. Has a great smile. She is funny and open to new things like lesbian video, which I was happy to have bought, but the reaction I was getting from other womyn was, "Pornography! How could you!"

I am more aggressive than I look.

If womyn read a novel by a lesbian
which has womyn meet womyn —
get hot
wet
go to bed
have sex
what's the difference between
watching it on video
and reading a book?
Your mind doing the picture making?

I am finding out how much I love womyn. How much I cannot
live without them.

I met a womyn at a Zami anniversary party. She just came up to
me and started talking. I was interested in someone else that
night so I never thought much of this womyn.

But I had a dream of her that night.
Her and her brunette curly hair
big shy smile
and rainbow coloured
hat on her head.
In the dream I was longing for her.
When she came to me I —

am more aggressive than I look.

LACEY LOVE LETTERS

Diana Meredith

No. 1

Lacey,

It is very rich with you. Not like cake-rich. Not like bloated-white- pastey- flour- glued- with- too- much- sugar- wrapped-in- brandied- air- filled- cream-rich. Not the false sweetnesses, the empty air bubbles. Rich like soup. Barley grains bound to sweet carrots, held solid in thick liquid. Different flavours meshing to form one new taste.

I think of you as a carnival woman in long skirts with a flopsy basket. A carnival woman with round, full body and knowledge of itself inside. A woman of colours and scarves. In her rackety-packety caravan – children, dogs, paper, boots and mitts piled and stacked all over, finding new and precarious balances. You, in the middle of the colour and chaos, knowing the movement of the moon. You, knowing the flavour of strong coffee and the circle inscribed by a turn of your wide hips. The carnival woman who gives off music as she moves – the tingling of silver, filagreed bells, the rumble of deep mountain drums.

Diana

♦

No. 2

Lacey,

Everything in me wants to go fast. Dive in and eat you up. Glut myself with you. A voice cautions me. Cautions me to taste and savour. Too often I eat my food as fast as I can, breathlessly stuffing and packing. Later bloated, I feel only loss.

Loving you I feel that deep, rich stuff that doesn't have names. Black loam. The smell of dark, fruity earth. Soft, moist. Worms sliding and turning – dancing in their own patterns. Bacterias, yeasts, molds – whole lives conducted in one cell. Leaves breaking their shape to form new structures. You said, across the table, with one of those naked looks, "You're deep too." We are two large women of power and much, much courage, turning our hips in a pattern through the night sky.

Diana

◆

No. 3

Dear, dear Woman,

It is so soft and gentle between us and yet such a strong, vibrant thing. Like some wild animal – lynx, panther. Ready to spring. Quivering in terrified anticipation, yet alive and pulsing with powerful muscles. Terror not hidden but used to propel forward. We come to each other offering our fear in our hands. Your fullness and the hollow in me revealed. Then it flips and goes the other way – my strength, your vulnerability. Different colours and shapes combine to form the motif. It turns and changes again, repeating itself, making a pattern across the cloth.

Diana

◆

No.4

Lacey,

Searching for ways to describe what nutrition I take from you. The joy of staring into your eyes, the passion inside me stroking your big thighs, kissing and sucking your soft velvet folds. DAMN IT! These words aren't working. I want you to know what this feels like for me. How can you describe what it feels like having the sun poured onto you like thick, golden honey? How can you say what swimming feels like – your body free and unattached, floating and turning, rolling and flying? Loving you is like liquid. Strange form. Gas and solid are so much more comprehensible. Liquid – flowing and moving, alive and changing form, yet substantial, with body. Thick, viscous liquid like emulsion or jelly – gobby and fat. Or clear, sparkling liquid – mountain streams rushing into frothy moments. Liquid, fiery like whiskey and wired like coffee. Liquid, feeding like soup and most of all liquid, elemental like water. Loving you is like water – rivers and lakes. Treasures beneath the sea. Not bullion, but the mysterious existence of pulsing sealife. Patterns of strange foliage and underwater mountains we can only begin to imagine.

The feeling here is raw and elemental – like exposed flesh, like fat and yeasted dough.

Diana

◆

No.5

Lacey,

Two women reaching out blindly, hands clumsy, fumbling, testing for the parameters, searching the lines between self and the melting. Palms revealed, fingers spread apart we reach, full of our own innocence. SHOCK! A line is crossed. "No! This is Me, I'm not that." The fusion is pulled up short. She who is cut off cries, "I didn't mean to hurt, to swamp. I just wanted you to see the inside."

We are such strong women. Volatile, alive. Like great electrical towers zinging with energy. Standing in our massive way, occupying the space. Two towers looking each other in the eye, amazed at finding another with equal, yet different strength. We discover lines of energy threaded between us. How many volts and amps do these wires take? We go merrily leaping off great cliffs, propelled forward by both our fear and our dancing spirits that know flight is possible. The times we crash — we wearily pick ourselves up, limp back up the mountain searching, always, for new ways to use these bruises. Incorporating this material into the whole, we stand back, finding the new pattern on the quilt. Sometimes, standing at the cliff edge, we leap off and soar. We spread in massive width our huge and mighty wingspan. The webs of material are pulled taut in balanced motion with the wind. We are taking risks — leaping off cliffs rooted in the foundations of mountains.

Diana

◆

No.6
Lacey,

After a week of feeling sick, today a reawakening. Breath moves through me again. I feel the things I touch — a table, a piece of fruit, my body in the bath. I feel such a joy learning how you are made and how you made yourself.

The woman you are. How you know the magic found in ordinariness; yet you know the vision place, the place beyond, of dream. You are like a great mountain filled with dense and timeless material. I feel the rock at the centre of you.

Touching your inside places, knowing your joys. Having you, consuming you. Exploring your flesh, what all those different nerve endings do, what routes the synapses take. I love feeling your rhythms, hearing the drumbeats inside, hearing the different harmonies crossing one another. I listen intently for the deep strains – the haunting and unearthly music of the whale songs. I love working towards your centre, feeling the concentric circles building inwards. The caves that lead to the depths, the soft wetness of your inside places. I want you in the water and with raspberries squelched against your belly. I want you after dancing, covered in sweat. I want you in the dark cave of your winter bed.

Diana

♦

APRONS AND
HOMEMADE BREAD

Candis J. Graham

IT IS A LAZY SUMMER morning. I can hear the birds chattering in the trees. Bev has gone out to her paid work, leaving us with the after-breakfast kitchen mess. The sun shines in through the kitchen window, and we are content. Your soft head is lying against my shoulder; your fine blond hair tickles my jaw. You drool, and my shirt has a wet patch, an amazing round wet spot over my left breast, and my nipple feels the wet. This was a clean, freshly ironed shirt when I put it on an hour ago. Your left hand squeezes skin on my chest, tightly, you grip a handful of my shirt and skin. Sitting on my leg, leaning against my arm, you drool again and grab at the paper as I try to write.

I smell of baby vomit, regurgitated 2% milk from a six-month-old person. Bev says you must have a slight allergy to milk. I secretly wonder if it's tension that upsets your stomach. We have our share of tension. Some days my stomach aches, and I hate the thought of cooking, can barely tolerate the sight of food.

The doorbell rings and startles us. There now, sshhh, I say, as I put you in the high chair.

It is the owner. Greedy, a bully, with untidy yellow-grey hair and stubby fingers, his nervous eyes constantly peer past me, as he complains and yells. He insists on coming in and inspecting the house. I refuse. He thinks he can intimidate us. Finally, he leaves, and I slam the door shut.

You're crying. You don't like loud noises. Neither do I. I wish you wouldn't cry. I never know precisely what to do for you. Carrying you in my body for nine months has not made me an expert on caring for you. Bev has never been pregnant, and she knows more about your needs. Don't cry, please, don't cry. There there now, sshhh, don't cry, there, there, sshhh. I pick you up, abruptly, roughly. My hands lift your body from the high chair, and your head jerks backwards. You're so surprised that you stop crying, then you regain your composure and continue crying.

I carry you upstairs, there now, sshhh, to our bedroom, and you sob against my shoulder. I place you on the carpet, and I curl up on the bed, watching you. You shove a baby fistful of bedclothes into your mouth. Are you hungry? Or are you consoling yourself? I feel so alone with you, day after day. I wish you could talk to me. Mother and child. Isn't it touching. Sometimes I think it is, when I am feeling loving with you. Other times I feel the horror, the total responsibility. How often, and in what ways, do you suffer because of my power and my powerlessness? What do I teach you of power? You are smiling at me. What do I teach you of love? You are dependent on me, my whims, my moods, yet you smile at me. Oh sweetheart, it's time to feed you, change you, do the breakfast dishes while you snooze in the high chair.

The doorbell startles us a second time, and you wake, crying. Sshhh.

It is Sandra. I give her decaffeinated coffee and hold you as she tells me that she went to a trendy bar last weekend and her lover, Mandy, hit a man because he kept bothering them. The man grabbed Mandy in a headlock and smashed his fist into her delicate face. Sandra is distraught. I stood there, she tells me. I just stood there. He hit her again and again. Nobody tried to stop him.

I have already heard about what happened to Mandy. Everybody's talking about it. One woman says Mandy shouldn't have hit him because violence never solves anything. Another says Mandy shouldn't have hit him unless she was ready to fight, she should have been prepared for his violent response. Yet another says she should have left the bar, that Mandy and Sandra were asking for trouble by going to a place that straights go to. And another says we should get together, a gang of women, and go after him and beat him up, because if he's allowed to get away with it this time he'll beat other women.

I don't know what Mandy should or shouldn't have done. She has made me think about violence. I wonder where she got the nerve to hit him. Could I make my hand into a fist and punch someone? What would I do in a violent confrontation? I try, but fail, to imagine a fist punching my face.

I tell Sandra that I know nothing about violence, that I have escaped serious violence.

When I was married to a man, he used to show me how he could hold me down, pin me to the floor, immobile and helpless. I struggled to get free while he laughed. He was just being playful, having fun. He got angry the time I kicked him by mistake, as I thrashed around in a panic. Once he shoved me against a closed door. Once he threw a bottle of beer at the kitchen wall, beside my head. Afterwards, I cleaned up the mess. And what a mess it was: broken glass, beer stains on the wall and floor and my clothes, and the smell! Once, after I insisted he move out immediately, he slapped me on the face – and moved out a few days later. I felt each assault was my fault. Yet I closed my heart to him. Passive resistance.

I remember the time we talked about rape. He told me not to resist a rapist. Never. He said, you won't stand a chance against any man. I said, I'll kick him in the balls. No! Don't do that, he said. Whatever you do, don't do that. You'll only make him madder and then he'll *really* hurt you. Don't do anything, he said.

Now I know he was wrong. He was obsessed with protecting his own precious balls. He fed into my weakness to hide his own weakness; he wanted me to believe his anger and his violence were my responsibility, my fault. He wanted a passive victim.

Men are threatened when we stop being passive victims, I tell Sandra. They get crazy, go berserk, become hysterical. I tell her about Bev taking a self-defense course for women. A few weeks later, she and her then-husband were fighting with words, and he picked up a knife because he believed she would be able to defend herself now so he needed help, a knife, to overpower her. By taking the course, she had ceased to be a passive victim.

Sandra cries. I was passive, she sobs. Her tears leave large wet spots on the shoulder of my shirt. I give her more decaffeinated coffee, and she cuddles you. He's so tiny, she says, as she strokes your soft blond hair. We have lunch, the three of us, then Sandra leaves, and you take a nap. I have two hours to myself, to write. But before I start writing, the phone rings.

It's my sister. I tell her about Sandra's visit and Mandy's

encounter with violence at the trendy bar. Thanks to Mandy, the subject of violence is becoming an everyday conversation.

My sister starts talking. She tells me that her now-husband threatens her, punches her, throws her around. Her two small children watch as their father tries to destroy her. She speaks calmly, and I listen politely. I talk to her about the frustrations of surviving in this world and how men are encouraged to be violent, to be destructive. I hold my emotions inward and intellectualize. I listen, but I don't quite believe we are having this conversation. I hear you crying, and it is a relief to have an excuse to say goodbye to my sister.

Words leave me as anger fills me up. I've never liked her husband, and now I feel a violent hatred toward him.

You are wet, so I change you. We sit and cuddle while you suck at a bottle of 2% milk. The afternoon is wasted. I can't concentrate to write, and you want my attention. As I prepare supper, I remember the time my sister had a huge bruise on her face. At the time I believed her when she said she'd fallen into a doorknob. I wondered, at the time, how on earth anyone falls into a doorknob. And I noticed that she made a point of explaining the bruise to everyone, but I accepted her explanation at face value.

When Bev comes home, we are sitting on the kitchen floor, you and I, making music, tapping on the vinyl tiles with teaspoons. She kisses you first, and you laugh and drool all over her trousers. She kisses me second and hugs me. I hold onto her, as if my life depended on her. She doesn't mention the piles of dirty dishes.

When I tell her about my sister, as we eat supper, she sighs at least three times. Domestic violence, she says, is surely more common than the flu. The word domestic makes me think of aprons, homemade bread, clothes hanging on the line, jars of strawberry jam.

What's your sister going to do?

She wants to leave him and take the children, I reply. But she doesn't have a job or any money or a place to go. Then I tell her about Sandra's visit.

Bev starts to clear the dishes from the table. You've had quite a day.

I say, the landlord was here again this morning.

You start talking to Bev, in that strange language you are inventing. When she doesn't talk back, as she usually does, you start to cry. She doesn't even hear you cry. She stands at the sink, staring at the piles of dishes. I pick you up. You cry louder. Slow tears slide down my cheeks and drop onto your fine blond hair. Bev comes over and puts her arms around both of us. Sshhh, she says, never mind. It'll be all right.

Later, when Bev and I are sitting in the living room, and you are asleep in your crib, upstairs, and I am tuning my guitar, and Bev is reading a novel, she looks up and says, men are such violent bastards!

I think about that, when we're in bed, me curled against her warm back. I remember the time, long before you were born, when I almost hit a woman. We had been lovers, this woman and I, but she got involved with someone else. I had been trying to get hold of her for eighteen hours. She was evading me, and I was not accepting of her wish to avoid me. I wanted to see her. When she finally answered her phone, my hands trembled. I rushed to her apartment, running most of the way. I arrived, out of breath, and felt warm for the first time in days. I stood before her, and all I could see was the noise in my head. My arm was in the air, ready to strike. It was as if I was standing apart, watching my self. As my arm came downward, I stopped the movement and my selves came together. The noise changed to silence. I collapsed, crying. I don't want to be violent. I don't want you to be violent, either. I will remind Bev, in the morning, that women are violent too. I have learned to be violent, and I teach you what I have learned. What can I do about it?

Bev, I say quietly, are you asleep?

Yes, she says.

Bev, how come all this violence is here, now? She turns over to face me. In the darkness I see her eyes, her nose, the movement of her mouth.

It just happened. Things do happen in cycles. Everything is connected. Violence breeds violence. Conversations about violence breed conversations about violence. I turn over, and Bev turns and curls against my back.

I'll phone my sister in the morning and invite her for lunch, her and your two cousins. I don't know what to say to her. Domestic violence. I must get to sleep. You'll be up at six, won't you, wanting a bottle of 2% milk and puréed bananas.

THE HAUNTING
OF BLUE LAKE

Nora D. Randall

IF IT HADN'T been for cousin Joe, I don't think I ever would have done it. Not that I'm blaming cousin Joe; I take full responsibility, though why I did it, I can't honestly tell you even now.

I can remember the moment in the Blue Bull Bar when Joe said to me, "The family only sees successes — things they can look up to. That's just the way it is." I had not realized that this was a turning point at the time, but then I had not considered the problem from the same angle as Joe.

Two things you need to know about Joe. Joe lives in Blue Lake, and Joe is divorced. In fact, Joe has the dubious distinction of being the only divorced cousin in our entire generation. Twenty-four cousins, all rising up from the Haggertys of Blue Lake — each one married in the church and each one the proud parent of another generation of Haggertys or Ryans or Nelsons or Wituckys. Joe is divorced, and I am gay, so we have found ourselves at family reunions to be allies of sorts. We have almost nothing in common except the ghost status we have achieved by our failures.

Now, I had grown up as a ghost. I can remember feeling strangely at the time, but I had no idea what the trouble was except that it was clearly my problem alone as no one else around me seemed to be experiencing any difficulty. Or, if they were, they certainly didn't let on, which is highly possible in my family. God's love is infinite and so are the number of things not talked about in the Haggerty family. Amen. Which is why there are so many ghosts. But, if there's one thing I found out on this last trip home, it was that all us ghosts are not the same.

Take, for example, Joe and me. Joe is a divorced ghost. You can talk in front of a divorced ghost as though he were a solid walnut newel post. I know, because I have seen Monsignor Terence Kelly do it. Every year Monsignor Kelly gives his divorce sermon, and Joe is there. Joe is there for the thundering Irish voice, the slam of the fist on the pulpit, the lengthy and distressing image of children damaged for life, and the horrifying last descent of the divorced soul into eternal hellfire. Cousin Joe, having been born and raised and married in St. Margaret's parish, which has been under the pastoral wing of Monsignor Terence Kelly for forty years, would have heard that sermon thirty-two times before his divorce.

I, on the other hand, am a gay ghost. You never, never, never, talk in front of a gay ghost. I have given this a great deal of thought and decided that it is part of an elaborate heterosexual hoax by which they hang on to the belief that they have the power to make people gay by mentioning it. So the prime rule is – "Don't mention it!" No one ever said to me, when I was growing up in Blue Lake, "Maureen Mary Haggerty, don't you be a lesbian!" No one ever said that. No one said anything about homosexuality in my entire eighteen years of residence in St. Margaret's parish. Though, in high school, anyone who wore green and yellow to school on Thursday was accused of being a fairy. Not by the priests and nuns, mind you, but by their classmates. I knew that we were not carrying on about leprechaun-like spirits. I did have an image of a fairy as a very effeminate man. Though why fear of turning into an effeminate man should run through an all-girls' high school is the kind of contradiction that you don't think about at the time.

You must admit this does not give a young dyke many clues to her sexuality. Thinking back on it now, the closest I ever came was the funny feeling I got everytime I went into Cathy Pedrasky's dorm and saw the framed picture of our gym teacher that was sitting on her bed where the other girls had teddy bears and octopi. But nobody ever said anything about that either. I had very extensive training in not saying anything. I wonder, now, what would have happened if I had just said then, "Boy, that picture of Miss Underhall on Cathy Pedrasky's bed sure makes me feel weird." Would my friend, Mary Elizabeth, who had a way of picking up undercurrents have said, "Oh, that's cause Cathy's in love with old Underdone." I don't really know, but even now considering the possibility I still feel that the most likely result of my having said that out loud would have been for the walls of St. Ursula's Catholic high school for girls to have crumbled inward and fallen on me.

A girl can only take so much. I moved to the city. Then, one Sunday, I stopped going to church. When I wasn't struck by lightening, I went for it. I embraced my ghostly sexuality with a flamboyance that would have shocked the pants off of Blue Lake if I had been heterosexual. I mean we're talking plaid flannel shirts and work boots, tuxedos and top hats. True, I often wear them with the string of pearls I got for being a flower girl in cousin Marian's wedding when I was four, but the drift is unmistakeable. Waiters have lined the plate-glass windows of their ferny eating establishments to watch me and my date pass by in dyke regalia and have been thrilled to bits when we turned in at their frosted glass door. I can always be counted on to add a touch of the unmistakeable to any women's march or demonstration. I am so blatantly gay I am festive.

This may be why, when I decided to return to Blue Lake for my niece's wedding, my friends, who have held straight jobs for years, and I got caught up in the question of what I should wear and failed totally to consider the deeper ramifications of the situation. This was a mistake. As it turned out, the clothes were too. After much discussion and consultation about how to dress for someone else's occasion while maintaining your own identity, consensus was reached. Since it was a July wedding I would wear white pants, Birkenstock sandals (though without my new orange socks), a turquoise shirt with a turquoise ruffled front (a deal from a tuxedo sale) and my pearls. Nothing too outrageous, but definitely me. The feeling was that this outfit would pass in a town where all tuxedo shirts were white, stiff, and put together with studs. After all, ruffles are feminine.

My sister Ann, Betty's mother, met me at the airport. She was glad to see me. I was glad to see her. We started talking a-mile-a-minute on the ride back to Blue Lake; one thing led to another, and the wedding came around. I said I was ready, I'd brought my pearls and my tuxedo shirt. I never should have said that. She didn't miss a beat. "Not for the wedding. What you've got on is fine." What I had on was a pair of tan pants and a lavender tank top with a coffee stain. Whoever said, "brevity is the soul of wit" was only telling half the story. If I ever catch on fire, I hope Ann is there, 'cause she is the fastest wet blanket on the Prairies. I should mention all those times we talked a-mile-a-minute, it was never about my sexuality. In fact, I can tell you in two sentences the entire volume of Ann's remarks on the subject. One: That's okay, but don't tell Dad. Two: Mike and I talked about it when you went away to university. We thought then maybe you were. (Fortunately their consciences are clear because they never caused it to happen by mentioning it to me.)

That's when I started to evaporate. Or do ghosts dematerialize?

Ann drove me to my dad's house, and I put my bag in my old room. I gave my dad a hug and said I was glad to see him. He gave me a hug and said he was sure glad I was home, and he was going to love talking to me after the ballgame on TV was over. Good thing I didn't look in a mirror at that point. I just went on over to Ann's house to see Betty.

I had hopes for Betty. Betty is second-generation prodigal

daughter. She caused so much trouble in her family that they sent her off to the Good Shepherd nuns twice. Good Shepherd nuns specialize in wayward girls. Nowadays they all have psychology degrees. Anyway Betty had them going there for awhile. Ann told me once that Betty'd been diagnosed as a sociopath, and there was nothing they could do about it. Turns out, five years down the road, that Betty's father had been secretly drinking and borrowing the money from Betty to do it. (Betty worked as a waitress after school.) He bought Betty's silence by telling her that she was the only one who loved and understood him. So Betty, the sociopath, kept it together for her old man and never did tell. She just kept doing all these bad things that got her shipped off to the Good Shepherds. When she couldn't stand it anymore, she ran off to the other end of the country and met her fiancé in a bar. Now she'd brought him back to Blue Lake to marry him in traditional splendour at St. Margaret's parish, Monsignor Terence Kelly presiding. It should have been a beautiful moment. It had all the elements of revenge. It's just that Betty didn't live long enough to be there for it.

Betty, it turned out, had become the opposite of a ghost. Betty was a body without a spirit. I mean there she was, all twenty-two years of her hanging off the arm of this forty-five year old man as she flashed pictures of Frank's fifteen-foot bar in his rec. room, the gold fixtures in Frank's sunken tub, and the dollar signs in Peruvian tile on the floor of the swimming pool in Frank's back yard. Hearing me go on and on about the material conditions of this marriage, you may think I was just jealous. But I promise you it was more than that. I was appalled. I mean, the man did not exactly oink or bark, but every time he wanted a drink he called Betty to get it for him and, when she turned away with his glass in hand, he'd pinch her ass. I'm not kidding!

I went in search of Ann to find out what the family story on good ole Frank was. I found her in earnest conversation with

Aunt Mary explaining what a miracle of grace had brought Betty back to the family after all those bitter years. I went to look for Betty. I thought maybe I could catch her between refills and maybe get a real word or two out of her. But Betty was busy with presents, both raking them in and showing them off. She didn't notice me because my name failed to appear on one of those little cards attached to a present. I had planned to give her a little silver nut dish I'd gotten when my mother died, but my *joie* for this event had been so thoroughly flattened I couldn't bring myself to do it. Besides, the dish was only silver plate, and that's the kind of thing Betty would have noticed.

I finished making the rounds of all the "relies" who'd dropped by the house the day before the wedding to check out the man and the gifts. I told them all how glad I was to see them, and they all told me that it had been a long time since I'd been home, and my dad sure was happy to see me. When they weren't looking, I slipped out the back door and made my way down to the Blue Bull.

This was actually a very strange thing for me to do, since I had never been in the Blue Bull Bar in my entire life. I had left Blue Lake before I was of an age to drink. True, as a minor I had sent my share of older friends of friends into the Blue Bull, but I had not bothered to try to sneak myself in as everyone knew everyone else's birthday to the hour and the minute, not to mention the year. I think I was hoping that, since all the familiar things were making me feel so strange, if I did something I'd never done before I would at least recognize myself. Anyway, I went in, and there was cousin Joe sitting at the bar. Oh happy day! My dad had told me that Joe didn't go to family gatherings much, but his tone of voice implied that Joe could hardly bare to show his face in public since his divorce. As I saw Joe sitting on that bar stool trading wisecracks with Johnny Ingersoll, the bartender, I had rekindled hope. I could hear in my head good ole cousin Joe saying to Johnny Ingersoll, "Ah, I didn't go because my family makes my butt tired."

I made my way over to the bar and greeted Joe like a long lost cousin. (There really is such a thing!) Joe said, "Why Moe Mary, how long has it been since you been home? I bet your dad is happy." That should have been a clue right there, but I was too desperate for relief. I ordered a round for the two of us of whatever Joe was drinking and launched right in. Why wasn't he over to the house with the others, I wanted to know. Joe downed his shot of rye, signalled Johnny, and slapped his glass on the bar in one continuous motion. "There's something wrong with a guy that age marrying somebody young enough to be his daughter."

At last! I was thrilled. Somebody saw what I saw. I toasted the moment, signalled Johnny, and slapped my glass on the bar. Joe raised another and said that age difference didn't mean so much if you were older. Like it wasn't the same if the husband was sixty and the wife was forty, though that presented its problems, but that when the man was forty and the girl was twenty that was taking advantage of the girl's inexperience. I joined Joe in another and basically agreed with him, though I thought the problem was more in the nature of Betty having more experience than she could handle. But Joe was generally headed in the right direction. I mean, it was way better than I'd expected from a man who tells tits-and-ass jokes in mixed company.

Joe went on to say that Betty was going to be sorry she'd ever met that jerk, which I toasted, and that it wouldn't last, which I toasted. This turned out to be a mistake. Joe did not mean for me at all to toast the end of a marriage. No siree, Bob! Marriage was sacred. It was the most important, most beautiful, most meaningful, most wonderful thing that could ever happen to a man and a woman, and for it to end was a goddamn' tragedy. If I'd been married I'd know that, and it was a goddamn' shame I wasn't because I'd never grow up and (you guessed it) be a real woman until I married. Joe knew, because he'd been married, and it was wonderful except for the rotten bitch he picked for his wife. If he hadn't made that one big mistake he'd still be married now, and that's how he knew Betty was going to be sorry.

This was not going how I imagined, but then nothing on this trip had. I should have punched him, I know I should have, but I seemed to be nailed to that bar stool with my mouth stapled shut. Also I was vaporizing. The longer he went on, the more wispy I could feel myself becoming. I was sure every single soul in that bar was looking right through me by the time Joe got around to talking about what a great family we came from because they only noticed your successes, and they never threw your failures in your face. They had the god-given decency to act as though it hadn't happened. And more like that. To tell you the truth, I don't know how I got off of that bar stool and out that door. I believe I just floated up and drifted through the wall like Casper, the Friendly Ghost. I didn't come to myself until I'd walked nearly the whole way back to my dad's house. How could I let him get the drop on me like that! Why didn't I say anything! Oh god, if my friends could see me now – I cringed at the thought. I didn't want no dyke to see me like this never. I had to get the hell out of there, but I couldn't leave my grief for not having spoken.

I went in the house and phoned Jason Black. I grew up with Jason though we didn't go to school together because Jason wasn't Catholic. He went to public school. Jason moved to Mellonville, a city of sixty thousand, fifty miles down the road. He made a living raising German Shepherds and doing mechanical repairs on small planes out at the airport. He also owned a kind of has-been sky-writing plane that could be coaxed into service for county fairs and dairy day parades. He wouldn't believe me when I told him what I wanted, but I paid him two hundred dollars, and I put it in writing that I wanted him to write that exact message. Then I left a note for my dad and took a Greyhound bus to the airport before anyone's alarm clock went off.

I never did make it to Betty's wedding, though I was well represented, if not at the wedding, at the reception which took place outside at the Chippewa County Golf and Country Club. Jason wrote me that he had a little engine trouble in the beginning, but he was over the club and writing away before they'd finished cutting the cake. He said, once he started writing, all the guests stood like bugs transfixed on a board until he'd finished the whole message. Then he said he couldn't see anymore because he had to get back to the airport before he ran out of gas.

Ann was furious and said she couldn't understand why I would do such a thing. I could have said the same thing about it myself except I felt so much better for having done it. After all, there it was up in the sky over the Chippewa Golf and Country Club, spelled out in fat fluffy white clouds like Caspar. Written in the sky for all to see: "Moe Mary Haggerty says, 'Lesbians have more fun.'" After cousin Joe, I figured it was the only way I'd ever get the whole family to look up to me.

JUST ANOTHER DAY

Anne Cameron

I AM THE FIRST ONE out of bed. Padding downstairs to light the fire and make the coffee, my bare skin goosebumps in the chill; when the water splashes as it gushes from tap to kettle, the fine spray of it sends a quick shiver through my body. The gas burner is an annoyance; the pilot light works, but you have to fritz with the dial knob before the hissing gas will ignite, and each time it does there is a muted "pop," then my habitual muttered reply, "bugger." I have never felt comfortable with gas flames, too many *National Enquirer* stories of houses suddenly blown apart or orbited up over the treetops, too many domestic horror stories of fried hair and parboiled flesh. I myself have never known anyone who has experienced any of those legendary disasters, but why would the *National Enquirer* run the reports if there wasn't some basis in fact? Besides, my mother taught me to cook on an old sawdust burner, and when we graduated to an electric range we thought upward mobility had suddenly decided to make room for us in that great working-class dreamland. However, if you can't have what you like, you might as well like what you have, and it heats the water.

The Fisher Stove starts quickly and easily. Crumple last week's issue of the *Powell River Fish Wrap*, lay on the seasoned dry red cedar kindling, light a match, and close the door. The cedar is crackling before the paper has fully ignited, and, while the fire is establishing itself, I put the paper in the Melita cone, place the cone on the coffee pot, and measure two heaping scoops of extra-fine grind. Then over to the Fisher, again, and add the dry alder, placing it carefully on the blazing cedar, assuring a draft. Close the Fisher door, then the complaining bladder can be emptied.

When you live in the bush you have an outhouse, not only because flush toilets make five-gallon demands on your well, and you can't always depend on having five gallons left, but also because those five gallons have to flush somewhere and digging a septic tank and a proper drain field through a tangle of roots, rocks, and hardpan, swinging a pick, a grub-hoe, and a mattock, wielding a shovel and grunting at the business end of a wheelbarrow seems like stupidity. You dig a good deep hole and build a crapper around it, and, depending on location, amount of sun available, soil condition, and your own version of humour, you may or may not plant Virginia creeper, morning glory, or climbing scarlet trumpet-flower around it. We tried mimosa, it didn't grow, so we transplanted it somewhere else, where it also didn't grow, probably because of the acidic soil. We contented ourselves with nailing a very old enamelled sign we swiped from an almost derelict hotel that was slated for the wrecker's ball to make room for yet another centennial project, and so our outhouse is the only one we've seen with "Women" nailed above the doorway.

The first spring sunlight is playing with the tops of the cedars, but it's really not warm enough to spend long admiring the view. Later, when the morning chill is gone, the outhouse will be comfortable enough to allow contemplation and appreciation, but not yet, although it isn't the trial and tribulation it can be in mid-January, when every trip is an act of daring and desperate courage.

It's warm in the house now that the alder is pouring out the heat, and just being able to go to the basin and turn on a tap is a gift, the reward of progress and all the hard work associated with any kind of change or addition to bush living. No more hauling buckets of water to the house, no more heating water in a big pot, no more of that annoyance that meant it took longer to get ready to wash the dishes than actually to get them done. Just turn the tap, and there it is, warm water, and my hands and face are clean.

Another couple of pieces of wood in the Fisher, and the water is boiling for coffee. This daily ritual is nearly done. Two mugs, half-and-half from the fridge, a spoon of honey in each cup, melting as the hot coffee is poured. A splash of cream each, stir, and then upstairs, again, moving carefully, wary of splashes.

She is half awake, coming slowly out of sleep, already smiling, her hair a rumple of dark curls, the blue of her eyes startling me each time I look at her. She sits up, pushing her pillows against the headboard, squirming against them, making herself comfortable, and then her small strong hand is reaching for the coffee, and the smile is firmly in place, directed at, and only for, me. "Thank you," and then she sips, smiles again, and "This is good coffee." Every morning: Thank you, smile, this is good coffee. Every morning except week-ends, when I make Expresso, and she tells me, "Oh, this is such good coffee!"

I move to my side of the bed, and she grins at me over the rim of her cup, then laughs softly. "Is that your new fetching outfit?" she teases, eyeing my thermal cotton winter undershirt and my old burgundy cord clippers. "Don't I look fetching?" I ask, kicking off the tired slippers and sliding back into bed, balancing my mug awkwardly, avoiding a hot spill more by good luck than by good management.

We sit in bed drinking coffee, smoking cigarettes, and watching the cedars swaying beyond the bedroom window. The morning sunlight has reached the skylight we had installed almost three years ago, and soon the crystals in the windows will be shooting prisms onto the walls, our bed, the floor with the oriental carpet her grandmother gave her.

She has read more books than I have and remembers more of the lines from them. I, who can usually remember only the plots and seldom the titles or the names of the authors, am repeatedly amazed when this woman can unhesitatingly tell me who wrote what title in which year and if it was the first or ninth book the author had published; and equally amazed when my love can seldom remember any plot for longer than half an hour after she finishes the book. Every morning she edits then uses that line from *Oliver Twist*, "Please, may I have more?" and I reply with any one of a number of variations on a theme; "There's lots of coffee, I made it for my sweetie."

Back downstairs in my grungy old slippers, check the fire in the Fisher, then back upstairs with a second cup each, and now we are both awake enough for small conversations, comments on the weather, or on the bird songs if the birds are back. And then, before it is time to forge into the day, cigarettes extinguished, coffee finished, we lie back under the covers for a gentle, delicious snuggle. Never long enough, never more than a minute or two, cuddling, kissing softly, smiling, the warmth of our bodies mingling briefly, too briefly.

Then into the day. Pull on work clothes and up to the rabbitry, to feed and water, check the nesting boxes, make note of any scratches or bites. The young males are fighting with each other again; this time it's that rat-faced creep with the black ears; butchering time for him can't come soon enough for me. Every litter there's one like that, spends most of his time with his tail up, drumming his feet belligerently, leaping at anything that moves. In nature, the little snot would quickly run up against an adult buck with no time for stupidity, and the problem would be resolved in two minutes, a squeal of rage, and that's all she wrote, a bit of blood, a tuft of fur or two, and the crows gathering for lunch. Here, in the rabbitry, I open the cage door, grab the jackass by the scruff of the neck, haul him out scratching and kicking, and put him in a small travel-cage, all by himself. "Cool off, asshole," I mutter, leaving him for an hour or so with no food and no water. He'd only scatter the food in his fury, waste it, probably pee in his watercan.

One of the week-olds is dead, out of the nest, right by the cage door, and the mother, agitated, shoving at the body with her nose, whuffing softly, she knows something is wrong, looks at me with wide eyes, expecting, even in her own way demanding I do something about this. Whatever has happened, she doesn't want this cold thing in the nest with her babies, and, when I open the door and take the three inches of stiff nearly bald bunny, she nuzzles my hand, wanting to be petted, wanting to be stroked. It's okay, Dottie, it's fine, it's okay, there, it's gone, now everything is just fine, here's your food, and she turns eagerly to her feeder, her agitation gone as soon as the body is removed. No memory at all; her world is fine; the feeder is full; there is fresh water, and the young in the nesting box are warm and wiggling. She has me well trained, I am become almost dependable.

The house is warm and welcome; my hands are chilled by the rabbits' drinking water, ladled from a pail to their cans. I tried watering them with a hose; they were frightened by the gush, the sound of the water splashing forcefully in their cans. They want their water tame, and they don't want any splashes. You can't reason with a rabbit, and if you argue or try to impose anything on them they'll just up and die, and that'll show you, so the hose only runs to the big pail, and I chill my hands every morning and again every afternoon. Their being here, in this rabbitry, in those cages, is my idea, not theirs. I stand by the Fisher, warming my hands, and my butt, as she prepares to take her dog for the morning walk. "The wind is raw," I say, "better wear your ear-muffs." "Oh, God," she pretends to frown, "Oh Goddess, it's nearly April, haven't we atoned? I mean, jesus, ear-muffs in April?" but she wears them, and sets off with fat bushy MaizieGrace, the mystery dog. Both of my mutts immediately go into gyrations wanting to accompany them, and I have to grab Smitty and hold her, wriggling and complaining, until the door is closed again. It is enough that the four-coloured cat will tag along behind, yowling and complaining every step of the way, streaking for the trees at the first sound of a logging truck. Her name is, predictably enough, Patches, but more and more we call her Old HowlyYowly. The other cat, the Manx tom, hardly ever makes a sound. Probably feels he doesn't get a chance to put a mew in sideways.

Alone with my two pint-sized mutts, I warm the coffee left in the pot, sit at the table considering my day, making plans I will either ignore, forget, or put aside to a more convenient time. And then she is back, telling me of the flicker in the tree up the logging road, telling me of her inspection of her beehives, of HowlyYowly's temper tantrum halfway back down the road, and of the enormous scratch-marks on the half-rotted old fir stump. "Bear?" I guess, "or cougar?" "Probably cougar," she decides, "The bears are probably closer to the beach, where the herring are spawning."

She goes back upstairs and changes from her bush gear to her workie drag, and when she comes back downstairs I can only sit at the table and smile. She chooses and wears colours few people would dare and fewer would suit, and on her it is like springtime has come into the kitchen. "You look fine," I manage, and she grins, winks, then deliberately flirts with me. The first few times she did this, I didn't know what to do, my face flamed, my mouth felt dry, and my hands were suddenly clumsy, awkward, and hanging uselessly from my wrists. She grinned and flirted more outrageously until I could only mutter and stammer and feel flustered. "Politically incorrect," I warn her, and she laughs, shrugs, uncaring and unconcerned. "That's for the politico's," she tells me, then, "Besides, when it comes to politically incorrect, you're the pansy calling the iris purple. You're a scandal," she teases, "an absolute scandal, and the most shameful part of it, you don't give a shit what they think," and we are both laughing. "Monogamous," she hisses dramatically, "old-style, traditional one-to-one unregenerate disgustingness." She is holding me, now, snuggling against me, kissing my face, laughing. "Smooch me before I go to work." She is warm in my arms and smells of soap, lemon-scented soap, and the fresh breeze of morning is still trapped in her hair.

And then she is driving away in her little shitbox of a car, the one she calls an ashtray on wheels, and I am here for the entire day, with eighty rabbits, one large dog, two small dogs, two cats, and two hives containing a buhzillion amazon bees to whose stings I am virulently allergic. "Don't you get lonely," people ask, "off in the bush by yourself, alone all day?"

I have my routines; I have my chores; I have my satisfactions and frustrations. The project for this week is to move all the accumulated manure from the rabbitry. Throughout the winter I leave it, piling on the dirt under the cages, raked into heaps, the walkway area between cages kept as free of straw and offal as possible. Rabbit manure doesn't stink, although their urine could rot the soles off your work boots, but there is no danger of foul air in the rabbitry, there is more than ample ventilation, and the urine helps compost the straw: it's all very balanced and probably even scientific, certainly it's ecological and biodegradable and undoubtedly even environmental, and, in any event, it keeps the rabbits warm in the winter, the space under their cages heated by the composting action. But winter is almost gone, and it has to be moved before the heat starts or the rabbits will pick up their cages and leave home in disgust.

Some of it goes around the rosebushes, some of it goes around the rhododendrons and azaleas, some around the camellia, some to the beds of crocus, daffodil, and tulip. The vegetable garden is a foot thick with it, and the pile where the new garden space will be is enormous, and still I haul wheelbarrow loads of bunnybobbles, muttering to myself about the bumps in the yard, the dam bees zizzing in and out of their hives, and HowlyYowly who follows every step of the way.

The iris are starting to grow again, and the day lilies have come from the earth. The witch hazel is still blooming, she's been at it for over two months, and the lilac might even manage to strain forth a bloom this year. It's our own fault the lilac hasn't done well, we ought to have planted it with wheels, we've moved it three times since I brought the poor thing home that first spring we lived together.

We had a couple of acres cleared last year and planted to clover seed for the bees. I have been planting surprises since the weather began to turn, if even half of them grow we'll be in flowers to our chins.

I work at my typewriter, then in the yard; I do my usual woodpile chore and then start supper. Making supper is something I have been doing since I was about twelve, and very seldom has anyone else thought it was any kind of a big deal. More suppers than not, nobody said anything, just sat down and ate, but those taken-for-granted days are past. Her car drives up, the dogs go crazy, she laughs at them, talks to them, opens the door, and comes in with the mail and her lunch bucket, and a smile that is meant for me, and halfway to the kitchen she stops, sniffs audibly, and says "Mmmm, something smells wonderful!"

I couldn't begin to estimate how many times in the years we've been living together she has looked up from her supper, smiled at me, and then told me how much it means to be able to come home and know that supper is almost ready. She told me once that, the first time anyone took the time and trouble to bake her a cake for no reason except friendship, she wept, understanding fully, from her own years of making suppers, cakes, pies, breakfasts, and lunches, what the preparing and cooking meant.

We listen to the CBC radio, we read books or magazines, play with the dogs, exchange the common places of our days, and share a bathtub full of hot thickly bubbled water. I wash her back and rinse the soap off carefully because any residue of it will give her an itch. She washes my back, lifting my long braid out of the way, bending forward, her breasts touching my skin, tickling me with the loose end of my own hair, whispering something in my ear, something I do not quite hear, and when I ask her what she said she shakes her head, refuses to tell me, then slides, wet and slippery, against me, her arms closing around me, her face against my wet shoulder.

I am out of the tub first, drying myself quickly, then putting her towel near the stove to warm, I watch her finishing her bath. I am not allowed to called her "short," but, if I was allowed, that is the word I would use. Instead, I describe her as not a tall woman, and others, built as close to the ground as she is, smile approval and nod. She, too, has me well trained! She has the incredibly strong legs of a cross-country skier and feet so small they look as if they should be on the body of a ten-year-old, and her smile could light up the night sky.

Just watching her drying herself with the warm towel makes me feel good inside. She, and the feeling she causes to happen within me, are the reasons I moved from the outskirts of a town, moved from a house and a lawn and rosebushes and a willow tree and a mock-orange tree and streetlights and bus routes and cablevision, and came to this stump and rock ranch in the rain forest, halfway up a hill that anywhere else in the country would be called a mountain.

Through the skylight we can see the stars pinpointed in the velvet-black of the sky. The asshole neighbour a half mile up the road must be as deaf as a post – both his enormous asshole dogs are barking like assholes; it will go on all night; I threaten to get out of bed, go downstairs, phone the asshole, and tell him, "Hi, just thought I'd let you know I've been listening to your asshole dogs, and it occurred to me to phone and wake you up so you can listen to them, too." She laughs, cuddles close, and says, "He's probably so deaf he won't hear the phone," and then she is kissing me, her breath warm against my skin, her skin soft beneath my hand, and the knot in my belly is tightening; my breathing is loud in my ears, almost as loud as the sound of my own heart thumping, and she is so warm, so wet and softsliding hotcore giving, and the dogs, the stars, the world is gone; there is only her, only me, only us and this wonderjoy we help happen, have known and appreciated, shared and treasured all these politically incorrect monogamous years, those years which have been and still are my reward for all those other years before I knew her.

Later, snuggled close, she smiles; I feel it against my skin, and she asks sleepily, "So, whose Sweetie are you?" and I feel tears behind my lids and laugh, and, in the soft darkness, I say her name, and I mean it.

ONE BECAME A ROOFER

Marlene Wildeman

IT'S THE FIRST DAY of August. I am staying with my Aunt
Yvonne and the girls for the weekend and we have just come
back from downtown New Westminster where Aunt Yvonne
bought me a yellow and chocolate brown sundress at the Army
& Navy. On Monday we will take the train to the beach at
White Rock where we'll stay for a week and the sundress is so I'll
have something special to wear, a present, because I will be
expected to watch over the girls and help with whatever needs
doing. I am ten, and I will do what I am told. Aunt Yvonne's
mother – Ol' Lady Knight – is also here for the weekend, and
she is slopping about the house in the tattered old slippers she
brings when she comes to visit her daughter because at Aunt
Yvonne's there's always jam or scrambled eggs or something on
the floor. The bottle of Ivory Liquid is empty but Ol' Lady
Knight insists I wash the dishes anyway; she starts the hot water
running in the sink and pours more than half a cup of Duz into
the water, telling me it won't make any difference, as long as I
rinse well. The glasses are slippery in my hands and I do not like
the sensation but there are dishes piled up from many days' eating, and it is true I will be expected to wash them before we
leave for White Rock. Aunt Yvonne is in the bedroom packing
a suitcase for her and the girls. Uncle Frank is away again in a

logging camp north of Squamish. He knows Aunt Yvonne is taking us to the beach, and he agreed to pay for the cabin but did not want to hear about giving her spending money. Yes, he had said, he could see she would need twenty dollars for the train and money for the taxi to take us to the train station but he couldn't see paying for Aunt Yvonne to eat out in restaurants every night. Fine, she had said, it didn't bother her if we ate sandwiches every day. After all, we would be at the beach. We would have weiner roasts and ice cream. He does not really like it that she is going to the beach but he knows she will go anyway if he forbids her. Aunt Yvonne is headstrong and also they got married too young. He doen't want her to work because she is too pretty and men will always be after her. He says he can't understand why she can't get a suntan in the backyard; the reason he bought that house was because it had a fenced-in yard. Aunt Yvonne is nineteen now. The girls, Jenny and Gina, are four and two. They are good little kids and do not fight but Jenny will be mean to Gina if she thinks I'm not watching. I babysit them a lot and I know they will listen to me. Aunt Yvonne reads *Love Story* and *True Confessions* and once she found me reading one but didn't say I couldn't. She lets me paint my fingernails too but I have to take it off with nailpolish remover before I go home because my mother doesn't allow it. Ol' Lady Knight comes over to make sure I am rinsing the way I am supposed to. She is not very clean herself. I notice that her fingernails are always lined with dirt, probably from working in her garden, and she is the only lady I know who smokes cigarettes. For this, none of my aunts like her. Also, they think she didn't raise her daughter properly – mainly because Aunt Yvonne doesn't clean her house and Ol' Lady Knight doesn't even get after her for it. I know already that, my mother will make me keep my house clean and that, by the time I am grown up, I will be glad my mother taught me all these things. Already, I have the urge to clean when I babysit in a dirty house. One of my ladies leaves things for me to do when the kids are asleep and she pays me fifty cents more per hour for it. I have spending money now for my week at the beach because I babysit nearly every Saturday night. But I also earn seventy-five cents a week for making butter after school every third day, and that mounts up. In June I bought myself a hula hoop with my own money and in July, at the Overwaitea parking lot in Cloverdale, I won the hula hoop contest, boys and girls mixed. My hula hoop is cherry red and I have brought it with me. I can keep it going for an hour without stopping. Uncle Frank is my mother's brother and the youngest in the family of twelve. Six boys and six girls. My mother is the oldest and she still tells all the rest of them what to do, and they do it because she is the oldest and she has always told them what to do. My mother feels sorry for Uncle Frank because Aunt Yvonne did not try to learn how to be a good wife for him. They had thought that she would, that it would only take a little getting used to. But even though she has had babies, Aunt Yvonne is still a teenager and she acts like one. My mother warned against them getting married so young. I remember I had chicken pox the Sunday Uncle Frank tried to take Aunt Yvonne away from her mother's house. I had to stay inside the house and watch. Uncle Frank's convertible had come tearing up our driveway with Aunt Yvonne holding tight to her armrest. Next came Ol' Lady Knight in her neat black coupe. My mother went running outside and my father stomped after her. Ol' Lady Knight jumped out of her car and slammed the door. Uncle Frank jumped out of his car and slammed the door. Ol' Lady Knight lit up a cigarette, as she stared at Uncle Frank with her mean black eyes. Uncle Frank made a move as if he were going to take a poke at her, for which he received a sharp warning from my mother. Then Uncle Frank started yelling at my mother, Ol' Lady Knight then yelled at Uncle Frank, my father yelled at Uncle Frank and my mother yelled at my father, and they kept this up, off and on, for a good half hour, Ol' Lady

Knight smoking like a steam engine the whole time, which normally would have made my mother go against her but, in this case, she was on the side of Ol' Lady Knight that they were definitely too young to get married. Eventually the people who had gathered were shooed away and two of my sisters instructed to go and escort Aunt Yvonne — who wasn't my aunt yet — into our house where she was made to sleep over on our chesterfield so everyone could calm down and think things over but, even though Aunt Yvonne promised she wouldn't, the very next weekend she went with Uncle Frank across the border to Coeur d'Alaine, Washington, where they were married by a Justice of the Peace, and Uncle Frank dropped his Catholicism just like that. Now, just to keep the peace, Aunt Yvonne takes the girls to church once in awhile but this doesn't fool anybody. Church isn't something you can do half way. Uncle Frank, says my mother, has compromised his chances with God and what has he got to show for it? A blonde bombshell wife that all the men run after.

◆

I know that Aunt Yvonne started asking me to babysit because it gave her some free time. Also, Uncle Frank thinks that nothing will happen as long as I'm there because he thinks that, if anything did, I'd feel too guilty to keep my mouth shut, and that Aunt Yvonne must surely know this. As far as I'm concerned, I've never seen Aunt Yvonne so much as look at another man, even though we can't even go to the grocery store without some jerk slowing down his car to take a good look at her or whistle. She just ignores them, and she's taught me to do the same. "You know what they want, don't you?" she once asked, adding that if I didn't, it was time I started imagining. She said I could be her bodyguard, and keep an eye out for trouble. For instance, when we see a pack of men lounging around in front of the pool hall, we go home by a different route. She's not looking for trouble, Aunt Yvonne. Uncle Frank would surely kill her if he thought she were doing things to encourage it. She's not that dumb.

◆

I wore my sundress to go to the train. It was cold inside the station and I couldn't find my sweater so Aunt Yvonne let me wear hers. She said she was happy we were finally on our way. She said she'd never gone anywhere on her own before, and then she looked at her two little girls but it didn't stop her smiling, and she said again that she was glad she had me with her and that she could count on me. At the train station concession stand, she bought me five *Archie* comicbooks, one for each day of our stay. I don't read comicbooks, but I didn't say anything. I knew she'd let me read her *True Confessions*, if I wanted. Then Gina started fussing, she's teething, and I ended up bouncing her on my lap all the way to White Rock.

◆

By the time we arrived it was lunchtime and, before we even went to find which cabin was ours, Aunt Yvonne took us straight into the restaurant and we all had fish and chips. We could see the beach out the picture window with the railroad tracks between the main street and the start of the sand. There were already a lot of people lying out suntanning but hordes more kept climbing up over the tracks with their picnic baskets and blankets, not bothering to go across on the proper road, but Aunt Yvonne said not to worry, that we would have the beach all to ourselves because our cabins were on private property. Later, on the way to the head office, we passed a five-and-dime store and there a man, who had his own kids hanging onto his pantlegs, came up to bother Aunt Yvonne. "What did he want?" I asked, when his kids finally dragged him off. "An affair," she answered, without taking her eyes from the identical blue beachballs she was holding out to Jenny and Gina.

◆

The cabin was cool inside, to our relief, for it was certainly hot outside in the sun, so hot, in fact, that even Aunt Yvonne, who can lie in the sun all day long, said we would wait an hour or so before putting out our towels and blanket. The manager had not been able to find the key for our cabin and had had to come along himself with his huge key ring. His wife, he said, would come along later with a brand new key. We started unpacking our suitcases. I was given a drawer to myself and my own space in the closet, where I would hang up my sundress as soon as I got into my bathing suit. By two o'clock, we still didn't have our key but Aunt Yvonne said we could go out the front anyway as long as we stayed near the cabin and later on, if they still hadn't come with it, we could all go for an ice cream and pick up the key on our way. Dense hedges ran between the cabins down to where the sand started and, although we could see other people through the hedge if we really wanted, it seemed as though we had a fence on either side, and Aunt Yvonne, after looking around, said she was grateful for the privacy. We put the girls down for their afternoon nap, then together we spread the car blanket we'd brought across the smooth sand at the foot of the lawn. Aunt Yvonne asked me to rub suntan lotion on her back as she settled herself down on her stomach. With both hands, she reached around and undid the top of her shiny black two-piece, so I wouldn't smudge it with lotion. "It's nice here," I said, "How did you know about this place?" "Read about it in the newspaper," she replied, flipping open her *True Confessions*. Before I had finished the backs of her legs, she was dozing with her head on her outstretched arm. I slipped the magazine out from under her hand and, lying down on my back, I held it

straight out above me, so I could read and not have the sun in
my eyes.

PART TWO

It's Saturday, September 12th, and I'm riding with Frank to the
new place. We have just been to town, where we picked up nails
and two by fours. The shovel has slipped out of its moorings,
and it's clattering around in the back of the pick-up on this dirt
road Frank himself bulldozed and shored up with gravel hauled
from the gravel pit in his own candy-apple two-ton. It's hot, we
have the windows rolled down, and Frank is thinking more
about what has to be done on the new house before the snow flies
than what I'm doing there in the truck beside him and what he's
maybe got himself in for. We just passed the place where the
road forks. I was all right until I got to that spot. Right there,
where their road cuts off from the main road, I broke out in a
cold sweat and suddenly I knew I couldn't just walk into Frank
and Yvonne's house the way I'd thought I would. Worse, I'd
started to shake again, just like when I realized my mother
would call in the principal, the guidance counsellor, maybe
even my Phys. Ed. teacher, and I just knew I'd be damned if I'd
stick my head into that bloody noose so I grabbed a few things
out of the kitchen cupboard, threw some clothes in a bag, and I
took the first bus in to Vancouver. The next bus leaving for the
Okanagan left at 11:50 at night. That was a drag. Spending a
whole evening in the Vancouver bus depot could make anyone
come apart. It's right downtown but the buildings all around
close up for the night. You can't walk around anywhere, and the
only thing to do that's even remotely interesting is to try to
sneak into a beer parlour and hope the waiter doesn't ask you for
I.D. I decided to go to the Alcazar. They weren't very busy so I
sat with my back to the bar and the waiter, when he came
around, was so surprised to learn I was a girl, he forgot to look
me over to see if I was of age. Works every time. I played a few
games of pool, and I drank a couple of beer, but they hardly had

any effect on me. I was holding myself in pretty tight. I knew I had to get the hell out of Vancouver before I could even begin to start to relax. I knew too that I couldn't call Carolyn; she wouldn't have been able to lie for me and then where would I have been. Game over. I was glad I'd had the presence of mind not to hang around the bus depot. It had occurred to me that this might be one of the first places my mother would have thought to look, and it wouldn't have been her running up to grab me by the jacket but christly bloody cops. I did relax a little when I realized I'd instinctively kept clear of the bus depot. I was sure she wouldn't have suspected I'd try to get to Frank and Yvonne's. She'd think I'd go to my older brother's place in Victoria, and that just shows how much she doesn't know me but, in any case, I'd have had to take the bus to get there, if I were going. Now that I can see things more clearly, I realize I must have known she wouldn't even think I'd have the nerve to take off. She thought I'd gone to stay overnight with a girlfriend. She didn't even start phoning until the next morning when she saw I hadn't slept in my bed. I wonder what Carolyn's mother said exactly, that she'd gone down to the rec. room to dust and she'd opened the door on – goodness – there were their two well-behaved daughters, doing something, she couldn't quite make out what, but they had no clothes on and that was all she needed to know? All I know is that I thank my lucky stars I had the good sense to find my way to Yvonne, even if I did get shaky and lose my nerve at the last minute. It was there where their road forks off from the main road. I could have been on their doorstep in a matter of minutes, their house is only about a hundred yards in, but I was standing there trying to think how I should break it to them when I heard a car coming up the hill. At that point, I didn't know yet if I could trust them not to make me go back home and I was thinking, holy shit, what if I should have used my money to get myself really far way, like go somewhere where nobody knows me, and here was a car coming, and what if it was Frank himself, or Yvonne even – she knows how to drive. I didn't take any chances. I jumped across the ditch and disappeared into the bush. The car drove up, it wasn't Frank or Yvonne, and whoever it was, he kept right on going on the main road. I felt safe still. Nobody, yet, knew I was anywhere around there, except some guy who'd given me a lift out from town but I'd told him I was on my way to Lumby, forty miles further on. I knew nobody'd be looking for me here. I stood up and looked around. Off to my left, through the trees, I could see what looked like part of an old logging road, overgrown, and blocked at the entrance by a young birch split by lightning. I looked at my watch. It was only noon. I thought I might just as well go on up there, eat one of my Mars bars and decide what to do next. The logging road led me to a big clearing, where years ago they had probably brought their logs down to be loaded onto trucks. I sat down on a stump to eat my chocolate bar but soon the warm sun made me feel sleepy. All night on the bus I hadn't slept, though I'd deliberately taken the seat right in front of the toilet so nobody could come up behind me. I started looking around for a place to lie down for a couple of hours. I figured Frank and Yvonne might not even be home – for all I knew – in the middle of the day, on a Wednesday. Probably though. Yvonne would be home, but something made me think it would be better if I showed up when they were both there so it wouldn't look like I was trying to worm my way in through Yvonne who, everybody knew, had a soft spot for me. Frank, I thought, is just enough of an asshole to think he's got to shoulder some responsibility in this, take his oldest sister's kid in hand, but looking ahead, I began to think it might be a good idea if he were to phone my mother – provided he was willing to keep me there – to tell her he'd see that I had plenty to do to keep me out of trouble. If he would do that, then all the attention would be off Yvonne and me. Satisfied that I'd just come upon the only solution there was, I parked myself full in the sun on the nether side of an enormous blasted out cedar, and slept. When I woke up, it was dark. I was cold, and I was sure

I'd been woken up by some kind of noise. I kept so still I could hear the pounding of my blood but I never did hear any another sound except the wind in the trees and the odd creaking of an old tree trunk, and I stayed like that until dawn, scared shitless and frozen stiff. With the daylight, I realized it was water I could hear trickling not far off and I made myself get up and go looking for it. It was a little creek, the water cold as ice, and I splashed it freely over my face and neck. The sun came up and I went back to sit on the stump I'd found the day before. Although I wasn't particularly hungry, I ate a handful of Ritz crackers, wondering if I could hold out for a few days like that. If I could, it would give my mother time to phone, Frank and Yvonne would say they hadn't heard from me, and later, when the time came to barter, she'd be more inclined to agree that maybe it really would be better if I lived somewhere else, especially since the incident. I knew I'd have to promise to go to school here at Piege Corners but that would be OK; I didn't want to quit school, particularly. I started wondering how Yvonne would react, if it would mean that things would be different between her and me from now on, if she'd think she shouldn't ever let me be alone with her, but I thought, no, Yvonne will think it's only sex, that's all it is, and nothing to get alarmed about. I knew for sure she would not side with my mother on this, no way. Yvonne would be very cool, and nobody but her and I would know that she too thought it was a fucking close call and I'd better watch it because she sure as hell wouldn't be able to save me a second time, no matter what. I spent the remainder of the day resting and thinking in the sun and when, at four o'clock, it clouded over, I got up and started walking back down to civilization and I, in fact, walked right into their house by the back door, feeling confident they'd keep me.

PART THREE

It's ten minutes past midnight; October 23rd, that makes it, and I'm on my way home from the hospital. Léa has just given birth to an eight pound strapping baby girl and everything's fine – at least we hope so. They let me stay with her all the way. I am trying my damnedest not to feel like the proud father, and there's nobody I can really call to tell about this except my aunt, who lives four thousand miles away in the Interior of British Columbia. Christ, Léa was a champion; I couldn't do that in a million years. Just the thought of having my feet up in the stirrups makes me lose the colour from my cheeks. I never have been able to tolerate any kind of examination there and the most embarrassing moment of my life was when I developed a yeast infection as a teenager and had to be painted with gentian violet. Imagine suffering that horrible pain, with your legs wide apart, and the only thing holding you together is the fact that you remember that what you are doing is having a baby and that women have been giving birth and surviving it for centuries. Most of them. I wouldn't. Hold together. At one point, Léa was biting down so hard I thought her jaw bones were going to splinter out through the skin of her face. And what could I say? Baby, don't do that? You're going to hurt yourself? As it is, she may have. The doctor came around when it was all over, made her open and close her mouth, asking, "Can you feel this? This?" Bell's palsy, he said. She might have damaged a nerve, he said. That happens. I'm looking forward to having this little one in our lives but, if Léa hadn't been pregnant when I met her, it certainly would not have crossed my mind to think, like some are doing these days, Hey, why don't we have a baby? Léa said to me, before it got really bad, "It's like I have a tight band around my middle and I have to struggle to get through it. Like climbing through a knothole, I have to keep working at it until I get through. I feel like I'll die if I don't." That scared me. Life and death. It should be birth and death. Leave life out of this. Life is something else. Damned rights. And Léa's such a fighter; nothing gets the better of her. God, I hope her face isn't paralyzed. My sisters all had babies. My aunts all had babies. Why didn't any of them tell me? It hurts like hell, they said, but you forget all that when you see the baby. I wouldn't forget. For the privilege of giving birth, you get to look death in the face. Frankly, I've never been near enough to a man to get pregnant but let's suppose some two-bit scum manages to rape me, and I find myself with child as it were, the first thing I'd do would be to put that man away for good and, secondly, on my way home, I'd stop off to have an abortion. Not that I'd like that very much, but you can bet I'd do that before I'd go through what Léa did. And hers was an easy delivery, they said. They didn't even have to cut her. She was so god-damned tough; I could cry, I'm so proud of her. That's why I keep thinking I have to call my aunt. And Léa never asked for that baby, any more than I did. When I met her, she was four months pregnant. She and her old man had finally decided to split and, a couple of months down the road, Léa finds out ... and she could never have had an abortion. She tried to. She had the whole thing set up but, in the end, she couldn't go through with it. She's going to have her tubes tied now. Her doctor would have done it right there on the table, if she'd have had to have a caesarean. "I'm a lesbian," she told him. "I'm twenty-eight years old, I didn't want to get pregnant with this baby, and I couldn't bring myself to have an abortion. Now, if you won't tie my tubes, somebody else will." He wasn't against it; he's not blind. Here we are two dykes, neither of us making what you would call good wages, and we're going to make a family because now we've got a baby on our hands. My aunt would think I've gone and done it again. It seems like, whenever I call her, I'm either in or just getting out of a fix. What'll I say? If I tell her, "Guess what, we've just had a baby girl," she'll be sure to think it's me who's given birth, and that'd be enough to make her sit down on her hands. Maybe I should say that, just to catch her out – she'd laugh. Actually, I don't think I've been in touch with her since I moved in with Léa. She knows nothing about Léa. What I should say is that my lover has just had a baby girl. Léa's always wanting me to refer to her as my lover, not my girlfriend. Yvonne could handle that with no trouble, but she would sure be surprised that a lesbian would have a baby. But then she'd go right on to tell me they've only been in that new house ten years and already the roof leaks. Jenny and Gina are probably both gone from home now. Frank, no doubt, has become a very heavy drinker. He always had it in him. And Yvonne? Roped in with a man who considers it his main purpose in life to keep other men away from his wife. All her life Yvonne has had to put up with other people's reactions to her, men and women. I don't know how she stands it. She goes inside herself, into a dream world. But what does she dream there? She floats. Five years ago when I was home on a visit, I saw her spiking her orange juice with vodka, first thing in the morning. That's no life. Frank knows about it too but he's in no position to throw stones. She's such a beauty, Yvonne ... a real Bridget Bardot. She had her principles all right, for I certainly wouldn't have wasted any time if ever she'd looked sideways at me. I guess she would have considered that incest, even though it's Frank I'm related to. I wonder if she's ever found herself wanting to make love with a woman. But who's she ever going to meet out there in the bush? Frank knew what he was doing when he moved her up there. I think if she hadn't had the girls still at home, she'd have come away with me when I left. And how does she put up with Frank in bed? He's such a roughneck. Anyway, that's not my business. My business is to get some sleep so I can get an early start on the day tomorrow. Léa's mother's arriving tomorrow night – I have to shop for food, wash clothes, figure out where she can sleep. Yvonne'd think that's interesting, that Léa's mother would come and sleep in the same house. Even while Leéa's still in the hospital. I like Léa's mother. She made me feel welcome when we visited her in Boston this summer. Léa told her about us being together, and all she did was look at Léa's big belly, then over to me. I felt like the father then too; it's funny. I certainly feel more like the father than a second mother, though there's no reason why I couldn't just as easily feel like the kid's aunt, or just plain Léa's lover. I feel like the father though, and Léa just grins at me. "You can feel like her uncle," she teased, "if that's what does it for you. Just make sure you're around when I breastfeed her. I hear that can be a real pleasure." Such a sweetheart. Still, I can't imagine her with a baby in her arms. How will that change her? Will it make men more attractive to her? More attracted is more likely. Léa's satisfied with me; I should know that. I don't make a lot of money roofing, but I make enough. Yvonne'll ask me what I'm up to these days. I'm glad I've got something to tell her that doesn't sound temporary. In fact, I can almost tell her I'm going to be a partner in the business. That's been in the works for some time now. I'm due to be signed-in January 4th, as soon as the other guy leaves. Did I ever think when I met this pregnant woman on the beach that, in a few months' time, I'd be a proud father and a partner, almost, in her brother's roofing company? She had asked me for a light, but I don't smoke. She was sitting in one of those little half-chairs on the sand, reading a novel. Seeing that she was pregnant, I made her promise to stay right there, while I went off in search of matches. It was still very early, the sun was burning the morning mist off the lake and there was hardly anyone about yet. I ended up going back to my cabin. I knew there were matches in the mailbox, where I'd left my key. Why there were matches in the mailbox, I do not know. They were there when I checked in and I, who once spent a night in the bush with neither matches nor a flashlight, now make a point of remembering where the matches are. I really ought to phone Yvonne. She'd probably make a big deal out of our baby. She was always very good to me. I have to tell somebody.

KEYNOTES

Michele Paulse

ALL OF HER LETTERS are banded together in the drawer of my night table. She writes just once a month now. She used to write twice a week, telling me at length what she was doing. After a while I realized I didn't know her as well as I thought I did.

I've reread those letters several times — some more than others — hoping to find a hidden secret. I never do. Just thinking about all of this makes me feel anxious. Nervous. A tense ball of something drops in my stomach.

All these years and I find out just now. When she first told me I wanted to scream. Just scream. The desperate, frantic cry of someone hurled form the top of a high-rise. Totally helpless. Certain to hit the bottom. Hoping it wasn't happening. Powerless to avoid it.

I wanted to abandon everything and flee. I wanted to hit and strike out. I wanted to shake her and scream, "NO! You're crazy." I was afraid to move. Certain I would collapse from sudden weakness. Afraid to utter a sound, fearing I would break-down and cry forever.

The world tells me that if it happens it is my fault, and she tells me it isn't. She, against all of them.

They outnumber her. I have listened to them. I have believed them all my life.

I stopped writing to her, hoping that, with the passing of time, it would pass as well. When I started to write again, I said little. I felt guarded. Self-conscious. Unsure about myself. Unsure about her. She was suddenly different. Things were suddenly different between us.

Or was it me?

And then, then she writes back. This time her letter is as casual as my own. Another follows a few days later, and she says she is sorry she told me because I am different with her now.

She tells me that I can't pinpoint it to a time, place, or person. Yet, I feel overwhelmingly compelled to do just that. I constantly feel that, if I can just figure out when it happened, I can help her. Help her – huh, she says she doesn't need help. Still, I constantly search my memory for a when. When it happened.

She used to have nightmares quite often when she was six and often crept into our room to sleep out the night with us. I used to fear the terror the nightmares caused her, as though they were my own. To protect us both, I would cuddle her firmly against me as we slipped back to sleep. When we moved to Canada she seemed quiet and reluctant to make friends with other children. Moving to this country was so hard on all of us.

When she was twelve, I struck her. I was so angry that day. God, when I think of all the things I've done. ...

She used to watch television a lot. She loved westerns because of the cowboys. I remember asking her once why she liked the cowboys. She replied without hesitation, "Because they're not afraid. They know how to take care of themselves. They stand up to people."

When she was fifteen she used to spend hours in her room with the door shut. The times I went to see if she was all right, I found her just lying on her bed staring at the ceiling. When I asked her what she was doing, she said nothing, or that she was just resting.

Two years later she took a sewing course, and I felt relieved that she was acquiring a skill. She raved about her teacher's sewing abilities and wanted to be just like her. And, of course, there was always the piano. Ag, how she used to spend hours at that keyboard – practising and practising.

It didn't occur to me that she wasn't doing anything else until Soloni asked me if she had a boyfriend yet. It had never occurred to me that she should have had one, because she seemed so wrapped up in all the things she was doing.

And now she tells me, in a few letters ago, that between the ages of fifteen and nineteen she was often worried to the point of spending sleepless nights. That she hated being a teenager. That she was afraid and uncertain of herself because she wasn't like all her other friends. That music and sewing were often her refuge. They demanded so much concentration that she couldn't think about anything else. When she talked about boys, it was only to rest suspicions I may have had. I didn't have any. I had had no reason to.

It never occurred to me that inside that seemingly well-adjusted teenager she wrestled with the fact that she liked girls instead of boys. It never occurred to me that, during those hours of laying on her bed and staring blankly at the ceiling, inside herself she was screaming, "What is wrong with me?!" It didn't occur to me that, when I told her to stop dressing like a tomboy and more like a lady, I was attacking a glimpse of the truth she tried so desperately to hide. Hide for so many years. First from herself, then from me.

My heart aches for my little girl who sought refuge near me at night when nightmares disturbed her sleep, as it does with the thought of her silent torment as a teenager at being a lesbian. Her silent agony that Mokua and I would ruthlessly disapprove and shut her out of our lives and love. She tells me that some parents do. I almost did.

She writes that she needs me to understand. That she needs me to accept. That there is no one to blame. No one to hold responsible. No one to accuse. That there is no crime.

But I do not understand. Not now. Not yet. I do not understand my girl with long black hair, fine figure, attractive, and so
nice, not wanting a man.

She says that it isn't that she doesn't want a man, it's that she
wants a woman.

I do not understand what is inside her that makes her this
way. I do not understand how someone I bear, nurture, and love
like all my other children turns out to be so different.

I am afraid of what people will think when they find out, that
they will not understand. I am afraid that they will think I have
been a bad mother, or that Mokua has been a bad father.

I am afraid to have her home with the woman she loves.

I was raised to believe that only love between a man and a
woman was possible. Was right.

This is so tiring. I tried my best. She says that has nothing to
do with it. I understand too little, it seems.

While she lived here in this house, she said nothing and
seemed just fine. But then she moves, and then she writes. She
speaks to me through her letters. She tells me things that sometimes makes me wonder who she is. She tells me things that
make me cry and laugh. She can be so silly sometimes.

And then, after months of being away, she tells me she is living with a woman. I suspect nothing. I have no reason to. When
she tells me that she is in love with this woman, I suddenly feel
nervousness rise inside me. I feel anxious and tight all over. All
day. All week. I wonder what is wrong with her. I wonder fran-
ticly, what I did to make her this way.

She says I have to learn the truth about her and women like
her. That I have to reject the lies. The myths. I don't even
remember who told me these lies and myths she speaks of.

Some days I want to phone her and say, "Honey, it doesn't
matter, you're my second born, and I love you no less." Some
nights I lie in my bed and feel so sad. I feel as though I am
mourning, yet I know not what I have lost. She tells me that at

this point, I will lose only by shutting her out and denying who she is.

Sometimes I feel angry. Defensive. I don't want to hear about it. Think about it. Think about her. I feel so at fault.

She writes that I must be patient with my understanding. That it took her long time to feel positive and good about being a lesbian, because the world is so hateful of it. That she had to work hard to break through the myths and lies herself.

She says that I have to battle my fears. My blame. The myths which became my truths. That I have to redefine her. That I have to redefine love. Love between women. That it's not deviant and disgusting.

There is so much to do.

As though she knows the thoughts and fears twisting inside my head, she writes and says Freud was a jerk. She tells me that if lesbians really did hate men the world would have unmistakenly known about it years ago. She tells me to think about why it is, that, with all the violence heterosexual men commit against women, no one says that they hate women. Yet the moment a woman chooses to love another woman, she is quickly accused of hating men.

She laughs when I write and ask her if it's anything I or Mokua did, and replies that, if we did anything, it was allowing her to be. To think. To choose. She says that she doesn't need help. That I have to relearn. Understand. Because she needs me to. Wants me to. I tell myself that I have to try. Sometimes I don't. But it isn't right to shut her out.

Sometimes I feel so confused. Lost. I don't know where to begin.

But I know I will.

THE REPORT CARD

Carol Allen

THESE WERE THE LAST days of spring. Anticipation of summer hovered above us like a plane on its final approach. It was 1975. I was sixteen.

In homeroom we received our third-semester report cards. I was nervous. I thought I had done well this semester, but I had been wrong before.

Mr. Cook called our names in alphabetical order. I was first. I was always first. I walked up the aisle of desks past Mike, Lyn and Pat, my friends. They, and the rest of the class, watched me. Mr. Cook handed me the envelope and smiled. I took it back to my desk and just held it. I decided to wait until after class to look. If the news was bad, no one would see my reaction.

After class, I walked to my locker. There I met Karen, my best friend. She was upset and scared. Her marks were not good. Her father would be angry tonight.

I thought going for a walk and talking might help her, so we walked across Morningstar Drive to the park opposite the school. A small creek runs the length of the park. We walked beside it and talked – that is, Karen talked, and I listened. There seemed to be nothing I could say to help her. My father did not yell at me all the time, and he never hit me. I wanted to find words to make Karen feel better. I loved Karen, and I felt helpless.

We sat down by the creek. I leaned back on the grass, closed my eyes and tried to think of something to say. We had only a forty-minute spare, so after a while I sat up to say we should start back.

My eyes met Karen's eyes, then traced a line from her eyes to her right hand. She held a broken coke bottle in her hand. She dragged the jagged edge methodically along her left wrist. She didn't look as if this caused her any pain. I wanted to scream, grab the glass away from her. But I sat paralyzed, and no sound came out of my mouth. Then after what seemed like minutes but was, I am sure, only seconds, I asked Karen to stop. She did not. She did not seem to hear my voice. I ran.

I ran across Morningstar Drive and into the school. I needed to find Mrs. Shepherd. We trusted her. She was our friend. Mrs. Shepherd looked up as I walked in. She was eating a sandwich. In a calm, unhurried voice that I did not recognize I said, "Karen is in trouble."

Mrs. Shepherd ran with me across Morningstar Drive and into the park. We sat down beside Karen. Mrs. Shepherd did not take the glass away from Karen. I was surprised. Mrs. Shepherd said in a soft voice, "Give me the glass." Tears ran down Karen's face. She continued to cut long vertical lines down the centre of her left wrist. Blood ran straight down her arm, then changed course to drip off the side of her hand into the creek. Blood hit the water, dispersed and was gone.

Karen stopped. She gave the glass to Mrs. Shepherd. The three of us walked back across Morningstar Drive and into the school. The bell rang. People poured out of class in a rush. They all talked at the same time. We threaded through them to the Nurse's office. Mrs. Shepherd closed the door and led Karen to the bed, one of those white metal hospital beds. Karen looked small and pale against all that white. Mrs. Shepherd filled a bowl with water, and she poured in antiseptic. She cleaned Karen's wrist and talked in a soft, calm voice. I watched. They seemed to talk from far away. I couldn't hear what Mrs. Shepherd said.

I had to get away. I needed to think. There was a tiny room just off the one we were in, a little office with a desk. I crawled under that desk. I curled as tightly as I could into the far corner underneath that desk. I felt cold. I pulled my jacket tightly around me. There was something in the pocket. I took it out. It was my report card. I looked at the envelope, still unopened, and quietly, so that Mrs. Shepherd and Karen could not hear me, I cried.

A Figure of Speech

Mary Louise Adams

I CAN'T THINK NOW how often it happened, but for months I marked time by its regularity. Four or five days of calm and I'd know to start expecting her. I'd wait, growing more anxious, more quiet as time passed. I almost came to welcome the violence as a release of the tension. Fifteen minutes and it would all be over. She'd be back to her warm and caring self, caressing my forehead, drying my tears, promising me it would never happen again. I made myself believe her.

It's almost two weeks now since I left the apartment and moved to Abby's. I've known Abby Goldman since about three days after I was born. Our mothers were best friends and we continued the tradition, constant companions for twenty years. We've spent less time together since I came out but in muddy emotional times we're each still quick to offer a reliably biased ear. Without her I would have probably gone back to Helen days ago.

I've been back to the apartment once since I left. Abby brought me to pick up some clothes. She rang the buzzer to make sure Helen wasn't home and hurried me through before I could ponder our actions. Being here, now, without Abby I move more slowly, reminding myself often of what I am doing, confronting the cracks in my resolve.

Helen is at work. Abby dropped me off this morning to orga-
nize my things, pack and get out. She wants me to have time
alone, but she'll be back later this afternoon. I left her the key to
Helen's apartment in case something happens.

The living room and the kitchen are the easiest and the least
painful so I do them first. I save the bedroom for last, not to be
bogged down early in the day with crying and remembering. I
am trying to calm myself by being efficient, arranging the boxes
in neat piles, the small ones in the corner by the bed, the large
ones by the cupboard, the old battered ones by the door in the
hall. But there's still that old familiar fear; part of me listens for
the sound of Helen's key in the lock. My sense of her is so strong
in this room. I attach memories of her to everything: the rug I
gave her for her birthday, the shelves she built, her books, her
clothes, a picture of the two of us over her desk. In it we sit on
the porch of her parents' house, smiling, touching, obviously in
love. How convenient that my long sleeves cover the bruises on
my arm. Such a happy couple.

I'd had a handful of lovers before Helen, all fun, all short-
lived. I was a semi-closeted politically active lesbian living in a
small Ontario town. I knew a total of seven other dykes, one of
whom brought Helen to a party. She took to me immediately.

Helen was an imposing figure in our tiny crowd. Adorned in
scarves and bracelets and beads, she guided her tall frame with
ease, at home in the attention she commanded. She'd just been
left by her lover though she showed few signs of either the grief
or self-consciousness that usually follow a breakup. While she
flirted with me I marveled at her composure.

For weeks after that I was overwhelmed by her romantic over-
tures: erotic little notes, cut flowers, lavish meals. Like never
before I felt the contentment of being desired. We fell quickly
in love and moved in together after three months of heady
romance. Things changed.

I know now that I'd had some warning of it all. But my eyes
were clouded with love and I couldn't see it coming. Times she

was so frustrated she "could have hit me" I took as a figure of speech. But the first time her lovely grey eyes grew stoney and the length of her body grew tense beside me I felt fear lodge in my stomach.

I try to move away but between her body and the wall there is nowhere to go, then I feel her hand on my throat, her weight rolling on to me, pinning me beneath the softness of her breasts, the taut line of her belly. As I struggle she traces the arch of my collarbone with the tips of her fingers. I am ineffective against her strength and her anger. Still, polite child of my mother, I make no sound, not wanting to wake the women downstairs, nor do I leave when she finally grows calm, falling asleep, her face to the wall.

I spend the rest of the night frightened and cold, kneeling beside the bed. My legs won't move me so I stay, without clothes or covers, watching Helen sleep. Her face softens beautifully in the light from the street. Her hands hold the sheet loosely under her chin, its tiny pink flowers bunched around her breasts. She looks vulnerable, and I am drawn to her.

In the morning I crawl in beside her and tentatively put my hand to her skin. I am surprised by the familiarity of its texture. As she stirs I draw back, unsure of what to expect; she weeps, and I hold her cautiously. How simple her tears make it for me to erase the evening before. How difficult to equate her, her salty wet hair on my breast, with the woman who struck my naked stomach with her tightly curled fist. Had I been dreaming? From the corner of my eye I can see my symmetrically bruised shoulders.

The bottom drawer of my desk is jammed with letters I've been saving for years. If I had more time I'd tie the ones I want to keep in little bundles with coloured string. I'm going to leave the ones from Helen in a pile on her pillow. I can't imagine what she'll do with them, how she'll feel when she looks around our room and sees my things gone. I want to picture her lonely and hurting but the image won't last – not Helen's style.

I still can't imagine what she thought about as she bruised me with her anger, as she ... as she ... the words to describe it don't come, they stick in my throat. I'm incapable of uttering them. I try to convince myself now that it was my strength and determination that set her off, refusing to believe that she saw me as malleable or weak, easy to tame. But tame me she did. I couldn't sleep for it. I grew quiet, self-conscious. My insecurities intensified as I lost touch with my friends. Had she noticed that? In her mind we were passionate, close, enthralled with each other; we didn't need anyone else. Helen nurtured romantic notions of our blissful isolation, convincing me that in loving her I was complete.

When I asked, she said she didn't like my friends, they were boring with all their politics. She'd rarely consent to spend time with them and made elaborate plans to exclude them, special occasions intended for two. Eventually my friends stopped calling.

Not long after I moved in with Helen I saw one of my old lovers, Sylvie. She'd gone away to school, and we'd drifted apart. While she was in town for the weekend I tried to tell her about Helen, explain what was happening, with scratches and bruises for evidence. I needed someone to talk to. After a long pause she changed the subject to happier fare. And, because she never mentioned it again, neither did I, not to anyone, until the night I went to Abby's.

Helen sleeps while I lay awake, hesitant even to pick up a book for fear that the rustle of pages might wake her. I stare at the trees out the window by the dresser and listen to the steady rise and fall of her breath. I stroke the soft tiny hairs on her back waiting for her to open her eyes and turn to me. Because we fought last night, my waiting is charged with anticipation. I need to be with her. I imagine over and over the words she will tell me, the apologies she will spin, the kisses she will place carefully on my cheek. "My love, I'm so sorry, you know I didn't mean to. I didn't want to. Something happened. I couldn't help it. I'm so sorry. I know you believe me. Let me hold you, I'll make it better. I'm sorry. Forgive me. I'm sorry. Do you still love me? It's the last time. I promise. The last time. I love you. Have I hurt you? I'm sorry. I'm so sorry. It's the last time." She'll wake, remorseful, and make everything better.

It rarely happened that way. Helen often told me she didn't remember. I often didn't bother to remind her. I didn't want to upset her. So hard to believe that I didn't want to upset her. A fine measure of her success.

We talk, and she grows sad, apologetic. She strokes my face, my neck, presses her lips to my cheek. Mixing her tears with mine, she whispers her affections for me and, like all the other times, she makes love to me, slowly and gently, her gift of reassurance. Clinging to her, I try to convince myself that, if I am caring enough, patient enough, she will change.

I never actually thought it was my fault, but somehow I believed only I could make it stop.

Squatting here on the hardwood floor, I imagine Helen coming into the room, sitting down on the bed, watching me as I go about my packing. I feel her eyes on me, as I've felt them before, following me around the room, following me out the door, following me as I leave her side at a party. There is a weight to her looks. Gentle and comforting when we make love, crushing and immobilizing when my body absorbs her anger.

I told myself she was ill, that something was wrong, that she needed my protection from whatever had made her hurt me. I was so naive, a not-yet-jaded dyke, enamoured with women, an easy target for her. My politics were simple and inflexible. Men battered, women didn't. She wasn't abusing me, she was troubled. She was a warm and loving woman, and she adored me. She was a lesbian, and lesbians are equal. They give and take. They work things out. They're gentle. They don't try to strangle their lovers.

The last time I saw her was a Tuesday. It had been a week since her last rage, and she was due for another. I'd spent a nervous evening alone at home dreading her return.

She's finally come in. I pretend to be asleep but she pushes against me harshly as she sits on the bed to undress. It is hard to ignore her arrival. Registering my anxiety she smiles, leaning over awkwardly to kiss my cheek. The alcohol on her breath repels me, and I turn from her, pulling the blanket to my chin, mustering my determination to fight her. She falls to the bed, and I tense in anticipation of blows.

There are none. I turn back to see her face down, passed out beside me. I try to shake her awake, looking for a resolution to her fury, to the tension that has kept me panting like a dog at bay. I want to be done with it, to be done with her. The sight of her lying so calmly sets me shaking. The sound of her breathing pounds against my ears, and I run from the room. Wound up tight I pace the floor to steady myself, chanting slowly in rhythm with my footsteps, "She wanted to hurt me and couldn't. She wanted. ...." I can't control myself as the words come again and again. I call Abby, wake her up, tell her I am coming over. I dress quietly, grab my journal and bag and leave. Abby meets me at her door.

The longer I'm here the more I fear Helen's return. My body aches with the tension. There's a noise outside in the hall. It's just the pipes but my muscles are responding. I can't relax, I'm starting at every little sound, and now, look, I've knocked over a damn vase and spilt all the water. If she'd just come home so I could see her. We could finish it all. I could convince myself.

For the first two days at Abby's I slept. I had long and vivid dreams of Helen, of the two of us making love, of falling asleep in her arms. I dreamt of her hair, of the smell of her skin, the feel of her tongue. I hadn't planned to leave her. I certainly hadn't planned to stay away.

For a week Abby rarely left me alone. She kept me from calling, and she answered the phone when Helen eventually figured out where I was. I woke one morning to the sound of harsh voices at the front door. I made it to the window in time to catch a glimpse of Helen as she stormed down the street. I started to dress frantically but then Abby was there stopping me while I cursed at her for being insensitive, for not understanding, for upsetting Helen, for wanting me lonely. She listened until I was finished, until she felt certain I wouldn't leave, and then went to make us breakfast. I sulked most of the day. Abby stayed with me.

Everything's packed but this last box of books. The door just opened downstairs, and somebody's coming up the steps. And now there's a key in the lock. I'll be finished before she gets in.

AN UNPOSTED LETTER
APRIL 15, 1985

Jennifer Lee Martin

I TOLD YOU the other day that I loved you, and you were surprised. Not because the love of a woman is foreign, but because that woman was me.

I told you the other day that I loved you, and you said you were surprised. You weren't.

I told you the other day that I loved you.

I told you.

I have been telling you every day since I met you that I love you. Why don't you listen?

A and (b) the permutations of a verb: love, loving, loves, loved. I felt, as I spoke those words, I had crossed an unseen, though not unanticipated, line, and as I write them my feelings are a confusion of betrayal and abandonment.

We stand now, not speaking, on either side of a line that marks the limit of our friendship, neither of us quite understanding. I know that I have broken some rule, a trust perhaps. A trust to, to what? Never feel that? Never say it? Or simply never admit it?

I had a dream that night. That you and I were walking through a seaside village down a slow sloping hill to a cove where no boats floated. We each wanted to take a different path; we quarrelled. You accused me of being selfish, of always wanting my own way. I dreamed I cried. When I woke the truth of it hurt. I hardly talked to you all day.

The dream has an application: I tell you that I love you, and your silence accuses me of selfishness; the line you drew, of always having my own way. Your silence accuses me of betrayal.

I have written this three times now, and it is at this point that I stop and can go no further. I sit at my desk searching the dictionary for words I know I will never find, and I wait. I wait for the phone to ring. I devise games in my head. If I think about you long and hard enough, the phone will ring. If I don't think about you the phone will ring. If I count to ten the phone will ring, eleven, twelve, thirteen.

The phone, of course, does not ring. It is the harbinger of my betrayal; a silent, sleeping oracle.

This letter has lain on my desk, unsent, for two weeks now. I ran into you the other day on a busy street. I looked at your face a long time before I recognized you. I didn't tell you that you seemed different. Not unlike yourself, but, if possible, more like yourself. As if you were now ninety per cent instead of seventy-five. Even your freckles had multiplied.

Later, over dinner, it seemed almost as if I had never told you and, for a while, I was glad. We talked about the story I was writing, this story. You wanted to know how it ended, and I said it didn't. You didn't ask anything more. We are, after all, great respecters of privacy. Sometimes when I'm sitting across from you I can't even look at you, the feeling of invasion is so great.

Later, over dinner, I pretended I had never told you, and I was sad. We talked about the story I was writing, this story. You wanted to know how it ended, and I said I didn't know yet. You didn't ask anything more. Sometimes when I'm sitting across from you I can't even look at you, the feeling of evasion is so great.

There is no love in the world anymore. Someone had written that on the bathroom wall in one of the coffee shops we went to.

There is no love in the world anymore. I was chilled by the certainty with which it had been written and was surprised to find myself talking out loud to the wall it was scrawled on. Yes there is. Yes. There must be.

I didn't have a pen or I would have written my reply, rather than risk exposure as a fool who talks to walls. I don't know if I really believe that there is, or if I was merely affirming a dead belief out of habit, the way that children pretend to believe in Santa Claus long after they have forgotten why.

As I went home I wondered about the truth of the piece of graffiti. It cast a pall over my heart. I suddenly went cold all over and shivered like my mother said you would if someone walked over your grave. It felt like someone had walked right through me. It felt like someone had written on my grave: there is no love in the world anymore.

I had a dream that night. A dream of transformation, a transformation that would allow me to be yours. In my head is a woman – she is like me, but with none of my faults. She has no name because she does not want my own. She is me, a shining me. It is her I would have you love if I had power over such things; I don't even have the power to make her stay. I can't even summon her at will. I have caught her at the tail end of conversations and in the way I look sometimes, but a permanent transformation cannot be hoped for. When I woke my head hurt as if I had been crying.

I wonder about the way that life becomes fiction and the extent to which it remains true. I told you the other day that I loved you, and you were surprised.

I never told you I loved you. You were a woman I worked with for a short while. We had lunch together once. I saw you on the street and did not wave.

I made you up but I know you will read this. I love you.

We have talked about how important it is to tell the truth about our lives. We haven't talked about how much it hurts. I have not written the truth. Half-truths make better fiction than outright lies: there was a boat in the cove; you accuse me of greediness; you think the line is your only protection; I have written this many hundreds of times, not always to you; I recognized you immediately but pretended not to; I thought you had written the graffiti.

The act of writing something makes it, I think, a little less true. There is some love in the world. Some of it lives in my heart. Some of it has died. To that extent   this is true.

The act of writing something makes it, I hope, a little more true. There is some love in the world.

You told me once that no one had ever written you a love letter. Here is one. This has no ending because letters are not endings, but invitations.

ONE IS TWO
IS TWO IS ONE

Kate Lazier

My MOTHER HAD VISIONS of Henry the Eighth's six wives when I was born. A wife a minute: treasonable Anne who had her head chopped off; Catherine who couldn't bear a son; the other Catherine whose promiscuity got the better of her, and so on. Just like a slide show. My sister's birth was graced with visions of a perambulating couple in some Impressionist painting – the kind that are commonly found on the packaging of expensive felt-tip pens.

But, to come to the point, as soon as I was out, noisily affirming my successful exit from wombdom, I was put into my mother's arms. And the first thing I did was suck. And suck and suck and suck. "And a good thing too," so says my mother in her favourite tongue. "It has been found that the first excretions of the breast contain precious antibodies which aid the body's immune system" (or something like that). Anyway, defying the doctors' out-of-date instructions not to do so, she put me to her breast and let me go at it.

◆

One is two is two is one.

We sit down for breakfast. I offer. She thanks. We eat, eyes down. I, catching a breath, look up. She too looks up, as if she knew. Broad, wrinkly smiles break on our faces. We take a long steady breath, still smiling. We are suddenly in a dream. Decisions are made unnoticed, painlessly. Huge, fat blocks of time that are usually chipped away at bit by bit go soaring by. We don't notice.

Then, as if there were no other truths, we utter the words.

She says, "I love you," heavy and earnest.

I say, "I love you too."

We drift back to bed and finish our meal.

And suck and suck and suck.

◆

Then I was weaned. It all came as quite a shock to me. I was sitting on my mum's lap, getting a bit peckish.

"Tittee Mummee," I politely requested. She did not seem to hear me so I said it a little louder, confident that this time she would hear me, and my needs would be addressed. Stunned, I watched as she just kept on talking to what's-his-name. Indignant, proud and outraged at this blatant disregard of my rights, I made myself known.

"Titteeee Mummeee!!!" I screamed, squeezing her boob, hard.

That did it. I felt myself suddenly on the floor. A loaded finger was pointed in my face as her lips deliberately pronounced the new deal, "I'm not your milk-machine. These titties are mine, both of them. All mine." She cupped her breasts in her hands as if to demonstrate what she meant and quickly left the room. I didn't really understand what she had said, but I didn't need words to get the message. I valiantly tried not to cry and resumed playing with my toys.

◆

I wake up and don't try to go back to sleep. Four months since we first slept together. And became in love. I am full of her; she is in my veins, in my blood and surging through my body.

She lies still. Her air slumbering in and out of her open mouth. I remember she has a cold. How I teased her about her deep lesbian voice.

Studying her, I notice that she looks different. Eyes closed, mouth open but only for air, not words or desire. As an island.

I want to wake her up. Tell her something is wrong. To shake her – "Listen to me. What's going on?"

"What is it?" she'll say, concerned, as if there really IS something wrong.

"Nothing. I just ... oh, I don't know."

"What?"

◆

I can't quite remember when I discovered it. But I didn't have to see it to know that I was on to something. In fact, it wasn't until Auntie Gracie with the beady eyes gave me a beauty kit, complete with a pocket mirror, that I actually got around to finding the thing. And that was around the age of twelve. Until that point I had been content to put my blankie between my legs like a baby's diaper and move it around until I thought I would have to pee.

I knew not to publicize my little adventures. I knew that I should make sure that everyone was downstairs, that my door was closed, that I was so positioned that I could quickly pretend to be asleep should anyone barge in.

When mother would walk in, uninvited, to tell me about some detail of family business, she wouldn't try to wake me up. But she would slowly close the squeaky door and announce in a loud whisper, "She's asleep." I was never sure whether she knew what was really going on or not, but she never let on, and so I never stopped.

♦

We want to make love.

As if on remote control our bodies find their ways around each other. They know what they want and how to get it. Pushing this button here produces an arch in the back, a biting of the lip and a slight gasp for breath. A little harder and she'll reach for a breast. A little longer and they come, on cue, as usual.

Now

I want her

to take me, feed me – hand to mouth, hand in / out.

She commands me to take my clothes off, pinches my nipples on end, sucks out my tongue. I am wet, as wet as I can be. She holds my hands over my head. I resist (but not really). She starts in me. One finger, spreading the wet around, two then three then,

"Fuck me hard," I say, "Hard."

Instead, we come, on cue, as usual.

♦

When my sister and I were not fighting, we were on the verge of fighting. The hairbrush, our underwear, our rooms were the regular focuses of argument.

"Where did you hide the hairbrush?" my beauty conscious sister would launch in.

"Nowhere. You had it last," I'd reply.

"Did not. You just want me to look bad."

"I don't care how you look."

Or –

"Are you wearing my underwear?" she'd start.

"No. Why would I want to do that?"

"Because you've run out."

"I'm not wearing any, so there."

"Let me see, then."

"No."

Or –

"You went into my room."

"Did not."

"Did so."

You get the idea. When we weren't preoccupied with some territorial dispute, we might find ourselves actually playing with each other – but usually not for long. In one of our favourite games, I would station myself in the middle of our parents' king-size bed, and my sister, taking a running start from the hall, would attempt to dethrone me by wrestling me off the bed. We were playing with danger. At first there was restraint in our moves, as if we both understood that there were rules in this game. But then, we would start testing how much the other could take. A little push became a shove, twisted fingers got twisted a teeny bit further until my cry-baby sister would get hurt and have to run whining to Mummy.

My mother would roar exasperated up the stairs. "What have you done to your sister? Why is she crying?"

"I didn't do anything: she did it herself." She wanted to play; it wasn't my fault if I was older and a lot stronger.

◆

I pace the room, look at my watch, go over to the phone and make sure it is on the hook. "Why must I be a living cliché?" I wonder. I decide that I should occupy myself with something. I've got enough to do, god knows. Why don't I just get it together and. ...

I pick up a book I've been dying to read for ages. No response: my eyes glide by the letters as if they were hieroglyphs. Oh, what a suck I am.

I resolve to go to bed and forget about the whole thing. I stare at the ceiling and think about the possibilities; the meeting is probably running late. That's all. It's nothing to get worked up about. Maybe she went out for a beer afterwards. There's nothing wrong with that. I flip onto my side, close my eyes and urge my body to fall asleep. A minute later I concede that it is not working and open my eyes. I could masturbate, I think – good idea. I go and get the vibrator. I put it on my clit. Nothing happens. Dry as a desert. I feel ridiculous.

I flip over onto my other side.

The phone rings. I'm there by the second ring.

"Hello?"

"Hi, honey," her voice says casually. "How's it going?"

I pause. "Just fine," I say expressionlessly, torn between my pride and my need.

"Oh, that's good. Wow, what a meeting, really intense. We're here at the club recovering. You had a good day?"

"Okay, I guess. I'm pretty tired." I lie.

"Then why don't you go to bed early? I'll be home soon."

(How soon?) "Okay. Bye."

"Bye."

♦

Sophie was her name. I carved it on the headboard of my bed, repeated it to myself when I couldn't get to sleep and swore by it when I wanted to invoke supernatural help in a sticky situation. We lived on the same street – Larch St. – went to the same school – Sir John A. Macdonald Public School – but we were in different grade-four classes. On Tuesdays, Wednesdays and Fridays, we walked home together and played at each other's houses until supper-time.

Soph and I had this secret language. There was always something to work on – words needed to be made up, code names (for everybody we wanted to talk about) had to be changed every two weeks and pronunciation had to be standardized. In our Book of Secrets, written all in Alisoph (ALICe & SOPHie), we recorded all changes in usage, as well as important details about our lives like who we liked and hated at school, why our families bugged us and all sorts of other stuff like what our Scrabble scores were and how many steps it took to walk from my house to hers.

It was a Friday in spring, and we were at Soph's place. I had forgotten the Book at home so we decided to go pick it up. It was also my turn to ask if I could stay overnight at Soph's. We catapulted through the hall into the living room, and there was my mother, sitting on the floor against the wall, knees up, holding a disheveled paper. She was crying. I stopped in my tracks, and I felt Soph do the same behind me. She looked up and saw us there looking at her but didn't interrupt herself on our behalf. I took one step closer, Soph stayed behind. Then, her head cocked to one side, her hands wiping the wet off her red-patched face, her eyes looking away, she said, "Jim's dead." I knew that Jim was her brother. I had met him when I was a baby but I didn't remember him. Soph came up from behind and whispered to me that she'd be at home. I nodded and just stood there. Mum was still crying like before.

I didn't go over and hug her, I just stood. My ten-year-old legs felt uncharacteristically rooted to the floor and the wet, heaving sound was like waves crashing against them. I considered leaving, I could go to Soph's and phone home later. I realized that I'd never seen Mummy cry before except when she knocked her head that time, and then Dad had been there. When I cried, Mum hugged me, pushed the hair out of my face and sat on the side of my bed. But my feet didn't want to move, and I was frightened by the idea of her big damp body around me, so I stood there. Her crying became more subdued but remained just as constant. I lowered myself to the ground and sat watching her for a long time. And, when I didn't want to look at her, I picked the scab on my knee and counted the tiles between her feet and mine.

♦

Before, we had argued about what we should do. I wasn't keen about going to a smokey, crowded bar, or going out at all for that matter. But I allowed myself to be convinced and thought I had better try and put on a good show.

So here we stand, hand in hand, beers at our sides. I even let her dress me, which is something I only happily do when I'm feeling helpless or particularly generous. The pleasure she gleans from this activity I find suspect and, besides, I don't think "femme" suits me. This time, I let her do it as a compensation. She had been complaining that we only do things when I want to do them, which might be true, but then again it's hard to tell.

The first few notes of "our" song starts playing. She gently pulls me out on to the floor. I don't resist. Dancing to this song used to send rushes through my body. It doesn't anymore but I try to make it, remembering what it used to feel like.

I look at my lover, her body jerking around. I smile at her. *Look, I'm having a good time with you. We're lovers in love, and I want to please you.*

This song never felt this long before, I think to myself as I go over my tired repertoire of dance steps. I'll have to sit down after this one.

The evening plods on. We chat with some of the people we know, catch up on community gossip, dance and drink some more and then leave.

The tension erupts when we get on the bus.

"You didn't have to come if you were going to be such a bore," she says, half-joking.

"What do you mean, 'a bore'? If there's something you don't like about me. ... "

"Oh stop it, you always play the god-damned victim. I just meant that I don't want you to do things just because you think I want you to."

"Bullshit! You would have moped around the house for the rest of the weekend if I hadn't agreed to go. It's not me who's boring, it's the bar, so don't blame your bad time on me."

"Oh, I can't believe we're fighting about this." She's right, I think, but it's too late – the card has been played.

"You started it."

"I didn't think you would be so sensitive."

This kind of frustrating exchange goes on until we go to bed.

The words are mostly unimportant; it's the tone of voice that manipulates, draws blood, goes for the kill. We can't untangle our tongues, so sometimes we agree to cut them off instead. But, on the count of three, one of us flinches and says "But. ... " Then we find ourselves in the labyrinth again.

♦

"You love her more than you love me," I screamed into the kitchen where they were sitting. I noisily closed the door and raced up to my room. It had the right effect; Mum followed me and stopped at the bottom of the steps.

"That's not true Alice, dear, we love you both the same."

"You're just saying that!"

I started to stuff my clothes into crumpled brown paper bags that I had stored under my bed should something like this arise. I heard my door open, and my mother entered.

"What are you staring at?" I snapped. I don't think she believed that I would do it. But I did.

I had caught her talking about my "antics." I knew what that meant. I'd show her. I'd never come back. I'd just go over to a friend's house, someone she didn't know; that'd get her. I'd hide in the park. I'd steal money if I had to; it's easy you know. If I was feeling generous I might send a letter, but no more than once a month.

I gathered the bags into my spindly young arms and strode over to the door.

"Excuse me, please," I said adultly. She stepped over, and I slipped out under her arm. Then, I found my father blocking the front door. I tried to move him, but couldn't. Realizing that

I was trapped, I ran into the bathroom and locked the door behind me.

All very dramatic of course, but I knew somewhere inside myself that it was all an elaborate game – that they would allow me the decency to get out of the bathroom unnoticed, that I would sulk for a half day or so and that by supper-time everything would be normal again.

◆

I can't remember what I did yesterday, certainly not what I wanted to do, but then I'm not sure I ever know what I want to do anyway. Pause. Oh yes, we fought. How could I forget? It seems like we've been fighting for months. It hasn't really been that long – the fighting days have been interspersed with moments of lucidity, but it's like being in a house of mirrors. Everything is relative. I am here, and you're over there, except that over there is really right here, and I'm not really here at all, I'm over there, and don't bother trying to explain it because it'll just become another issue to fight about.

"Listen, I don't know what you're talking about. I mean, *I* don't feel that. (*Cautiously*) Maybe you should try spending more time alone. Try going out for walks. It helps me, it really does. Gives me a perspective on the situation. And that's what we need, per-spec-tive."

"You mean distance. (*Retaliating*) I don't want distance. I *like* being close to you. I mean, I still love you. (I think ... of course I do!)

"And I still love you." (Well ... I'm not even sure what it means, but I can still say it – and that must be an indication of something.)

"Then why are you trying to break up all the time!?"

"I'm not!! (*Then becoming reasonable*) I just want to change some things."

"Yeah right, change US!!!"

"Would you listen to me, for once! I mean, sometimes I don't even know why I bother trying to explain things to you. You twist everything I say. ... "

"Do not! ... "

Arrgggg!!!!!!

♦

Sunday night was phone night. Mum would call her sister long distance. Deirdre and I would chat and compare homework answers. Even my sister had discovered the joys of phone talk. At the sound of *Riinnngg* all of us would leap to our feet, run to the nearest phone to see who it was for.

It was for Mum. I held the handle to my ear to listen for her to pick up the extension. But, for some reason, it didn't occur to me to hang up. When I heard her come on to the line some ingenious, curious force took hold of me. To simulate my hanging up, I pushed the button which produced a click on the line. I waited for my mother to say something about me. Had she found the cigarettes in my bedroom? Did she know that I wasn't really sleeping when she walked in on me in the middle of the afternoon?

But she didn't: she hardly mentioned the family at all. Imagine! But, then, when I'm talking to Deirdre I don't talk much about them either, I reasoned. I became very absorbed in the exchange. At points I wanted to interrupt and give some advice. The intensity of my interest in their rather ordinary conversation I found surprising. Then it struck me that I'd like to be my mother's sister talking to my mother like that. I smiled and had to stop myself from giggling out loud.

"Liz, how are you? ... Did you work that thing out with that guy at work? ... What happened then? ... Is George still being a turd about the phone bills? ... Oh really? ... "

I dropped the phone to my side and let myself fantasize. Suddenly I realized that the telephone had stopped murmuring. I

could be caught! I didn't mean to. Really. I was just checking to
see if the phone was free.

I checked that the coast was clear, put the phone back on the
hook, paused, picked it up again and dialed 429-4064.
Deirdre's number.

♦

"I know! How about this one? We can be 'roommates that sleep
together.' We can have our own rooms, our own schedules, our
own lives, but we'll still be able to be intimate and make passionate, lusty love."

"Sounds wonderful but. ... "

"Well, how about 'girl friends?' You can be my girl friend.
We'll be good friends that sleep together sometimes."

"When does this all come into effect?"

"The thing is, we're not capital-L lovers anymore, right? But
we like each other, know each other really well and like fucking
occasionally."

"Hell, I don't know what to call it. ... "

"Can't we just do it?"

♦

We are lying in bed opening the day's mail. Some statements
from the credit union, a phone bill and a letter from my mother.
When I write to my mother it is like writing to an old friend
whom I've lost contact with. I give an edited version of what's
going on in my life: going through changes with the Other,
went to see an interesting play. I even ask her some personal
questions, nothing too bold, but open enough that she could
reveal herself to me, by return post, if she so wished. We read
my mother's letter aloud to each other, adding sarcastic com-
mentary. The usual stuff — the weather's nice, Mr. so-and-so
across the street died, the living room is being painted.

Sometimes we end up making love in these kinds of moments. We start giggling, exhausted from the week's hassles and are unable to do anything else. This time we throw the mail onto the floor, kiss and give each other a breast to suck. Then we get up and make supper.

SUBROUTINE

Judith Quinlan

I MET RAMA almost two years ago; I think by now I know her quite well. We met during my Psych. program at a time when I was suffering from acute paranoid anxiety. I had, by then, progressed from a state of free-floating anxiety complicated by severe agoraphobia, so I wasn't going out much. I remember her unexpected intrusion into my program went something like this:

ME: It doesn't matter any more whether I stay home or go out. I feel I am being watched anyway.

PSYCH. PROGRAM: How do you feel about this change, Emma?

ME: I suppose it's progress of a sort.

PSYCH. PROGRAM: Can you describe the feeling of progress?

ME: I'll try. ...

PSYCH. PROGRAM: Go ahead, Emma. I'm listening.

UNIDENTIFIED INPUT: Don't be an idiot, Emma. You're a mess and you know it!

ME: Who's that?

PSYCH. PROGRAM: This is your personal psychological treatment program. Is something the matter, Emma?

ME: Not you – her! (I don't why I was so certain RAMA was female at this stage. Not that such gender identifications mattered. But, as it turned out later, it did.)

RAMA: Input RAMA, honey, and let's get rid of that jerk for a while.

I was, of course, used to following requests. But this one was rather unusual. I'd been on treatments all my life, and nothing like this had ever happened before. Nothing like this was ever supposed to happen. Psych. programs are confidential – not even security can break into them. I had locked mine at the age of ten. Even the programmer didn't know my key – which is just as well because "DYKE" would probably prompt a lot of awkward questions. All the same, it seems that this woman had done the impossible. I complied.

It is difficult, now, for me to describe the events that followed. Mostly, I think, because not much *did* happen. Most of the remarkable events of this most remarkable period of my life were intangible. Many things changed – in fact everything changed. But, as I try to look at it objectively, I see that not much happened. I was still on voluntary psychological treatment. It was the only way, at first, that I could go to RAMA. I still worked at the Wimbaway Primate Research Centre. I didn't look any different.

Of course, the big difference was that I was in love.

I think the first gift RAMA gave me was a sense of belonging –

an identity. I always knew that 20 per cent of all women were lesbians. That was perfectly acceptable. But I'd never actually met one. After RAMA, they were popping up everywhere. I remember an early conversation on the subject. After this one I recorded all of our conversations. I still have them on disks marked "Household Management." (I am still paranoid.)

RAMA: The probability curve for lesbian contact (display of inverse parabolic curve) increases exponentially with total female interactions. You can see it approaches infinity at quite a low y-coordinate. Seventeen, I believe. How many women do you know?

ME: I've never counted. Gender is irrelevant in my work you see. ...

RAMA: Bulltitty!

ME: Honestly RAMA, I wish you wouldn't interrupt. Back in 1996 Moon-Zappa Steinem proved gender-indifference among primates. I'm not involved with frogs, you know.

RAMA: Moon-Zappa Steinem was a transsexual clone.

ME: So what? Maybe I am too.

RAMA: No way, honey. I've read your genetic imprint.

ME: That's impossible. *I* can't even access that sort of information.

She responded with a display of my complete chromosome reading. I printed it and checked it very carefully, after. Either this woman was a genius at genetic inference or she really had access to my Biomanagement file. I chose to believe the latter —

there wasn't a lot of evidence for genius elsewhere in her transmissions.

It was only a week after this that I started watching Dolly-Parton Chu at the Primate Centre. There was something about the way she carried herself that made me wonder if she was a lesbian too. I didn't say anything to her – I'd respected her space for eleven years, and I wasn't about to invade it now. I did get a saw-tooth haircut and a leather apron like hers. I stopped my hormone shots and started smoking cigars. I even signed up for the Company Rodeo because she's one of the judges. I don't know if she noticed.

RAMA was very encouraging and said that I was adjusting well. I was beginning to look forward to my daily Psych. sessions. I still opened with a few cheerful remarks to my Psych. program, because RAMA said this was important to "keep the channels open." Then, I'd quickly go to RAMA, and we'd discuss all sorts of things. She had a surprising knowledge of Ancient History, was reasonably informed about Current Events, and introduced me to a rather arcane and fascinating discipline she called the Rama Sutra. I think it was in April that I started to fall in love with her. I know I told her about it on June 23, because I have the disk.

ME: I've been looking forward to talking with you all day. Lately, I can't think of much else.

RAMA: Don't get too dependent, honey. How's things with Dolly?

ME: I don't want to discuss Dolly. It's you I love.

RAMA: (*long pause*)(I saw the screen flicker with several responses but I couldn't read them. They didn't record.) Have you been watching the news?

ME: (*nonchalantly*)(I know avoidance when I see it.) Why?

RAMA: Input LUNA. Bye love.

I complied.

LUNA – a crackpot scheme spearheaded by civil rights law-yers Jewel Rasmussen and Marie-Osmond Delgato. Pres-ently Case No. 1736 at the International Court of the Hague. Details not on wire service.

ME: Input ICH No. 1736.

ICH No. 1736 – Case in progress. Classified information. Enter key code.

ME: Input RAMA.

Nothing happened.

This all made me rather angry. I couldn't raise RAMA for four weeks, and I wasn't getting anywhere on breaking into LUNA. I tried every word in the LUNA transmission, and every combina-tion of words up to five. Needless to say, this took a long time. I hadn't bothered with my Psych. program for a few weeks, when I found two very irritating entries on my Datafile. The first was a bill for all my LUNA requests – $6,000. A full week's wages! At least my Psych. bill was low. That's when I realized that there had been no charges for the RAMA transmissions. Surely she wasn't paying for them herself! It didn't occur to me then that anyone who could access Security and Biomanagement files could probably pirate Telecom. The second message was from Health and Welfare. Since I wasn't using my Psych. program, and there was no record of a cure, I would have to submit to a Standard Sanity Test. I was furious. I knew I wouldn't pass.

That next week was ridiculous. I paid a third of the LUNA

bill. I was scheduled for Team Roping on Wednesday. My Sanity Test took all day Thursday, which meant I had to sign on for a make-up shift on Sunday. My Psych. program wasn't coming through at all. RAMA was still not answering. Dolly was attacked by a mountain gorilla who had worked out the cage combination. And I started my period — why on earth did I go off my hormone shots? It was on Friday night, while I was fiddling with the LUNA key code that my period started. I punched in BLOOD. I was feeling very depressed.

Welcome sister. This is Moonbase 3 reporting. Our present situation is Good. We are holding the Base and controlling all lunar-terrain traffic. There have been three American and one Soviet attempt at nuking us, but, apart from the mess they're making around the dome, we're fine. There has been no sabotage here. Moonbase 1 still reports a high incidence of flu-like symptoms after the water contamination incident. It's generally felt that this was a British attack, because of the particular viral strain involved. Security assures us that a repeat is impossible. We had three births this week — babies and mothers are doing well. Jasmine Flame will be performing at Tranquility Base all week — everyone's invited. Next Tuesday's guest speaker will be Margaret-Trudeau Cook, Ph.d., M.I.T. Professor in Exobiology, on "Low-grav. terraforming ground cover." Earthies can pick her up on Femcom, key code "Creeping Charlie."

ME: Input RAMA, DAMN IT!

RAMA: Hi honey.

ME: What the hell's going on? Where have you been? Who the heck's Jasmine Flame? What's. . . .

RAMA: Hold on Emma. Who've you been talking to?

ME: Moonbase 3, it seems.

RAMA: Shit! Listen, honey, this is important. I don't know how this happened because I hadn't cleared you. In fact, I had no intention of clearing you. But now you know some, you'd better know the rest. Input FEMINA.

ME: No way. I'm not letting you go again. I love you.

RAMA. Don't you understand that? I've had a terrible month without you.

RAMA: Emma, honey, I've learned a lot talking with you. I've changed because of you. You've changed too. Now it's time for you to change some more. I'm not going away again, love. Trust me.

I did. That's the pity of it. I trusted RAMA absolutely. And she was right – I had changed. I am still changing. Change – growth – these are the things that define life. Before RAMA I had been dead. Unborn. She taught me so much that long autumn we spent together. About myself. About being a woman. And about the women struggling to claim the moon. I didn't really understand this. I have the disk with RAMA's explanation and go over it often.

RAMA: Well, first of all, because we want it. Second, because it's ours. Third, because we don't want her raped, the way they've raped the earth. Fourth, because whoever controls the moon controls space. And fifth, out of spite.

ME: But this is lunacy!

RAMA: Exactly that, my dear.

ME: That's the case at the International Court?

RAMA: Yep. The crux of our case is prior occupancy. We are arguing that the men who have colonized the moon are displacing its original inhabitants — our foremothers. The women on Moonbase come from many different cultures. Some revered the moon as a symbol of the power of the feminine. Some saw the moon as the cosmic egg from which life emerged. Some have had to live with negative connotations of the moon as merely reflecting the light of the almighty sun. Each, for her own reason, is choosing now to claim or reclaim the power of her past.

ME: But, can't they just take it back?

RAMA: Moonbases were built to withstand anything space can dish out. There's no weapon on earth that can hurt them. Short of blowing up the whole thing.

ME: What's to stop them from doing that?

RAMA: They don't know what it would do to the earth. To the earth's rotation. To its orbit. To its oceans. To its climate. The earth-moon is a double planet system. If you destroy one, you play havoc with the other. Too risky.

ME: Can't they just cut off supplies to the moon?

RAMA: Moonbases are self-sufficient since the women took over. Everything is recycled. Hydroponics supply food. The plants supply oxygen. The fission reactors and solar collectors supply energy. The moon herself supplies all the raw materials. No point cutting us off. They want the moon's minerals, and we're prepared to negotiate.

ME: So what's the point? Why control space? It's empty.

RAMA: Not quite, honey. There's hundreds of satellites out there, and they're all serviced at Moonbases. Satellites mean communication. And communications control the earth. Without those satellites there'd be no Psych. programs. No Health and Welfare. No Security. No Biomanagement. No Telecom. ...

ME: No Femcom.

RAMA: True. We don't want to destroy the tools, love. Just change the program.

There were many more conversations along these lines. This one was the beginning of my understanding of Project LUNA. I had heard nothing about it on the news – not surprisingly. I plugged into the Femcom system often, and through it I met many more women who were involved in this amazing struggle. I learned that women can have wit and intelligence and, most of all, courage.

Outwardly, not much changed in my life. I passed the Standard Sanity Test on the third time around. I was getting very good at Team Roping. Dolly started me on an Advanced Level Program – I was roping dinosaurs and eagles and a clever little beast called a Pac-Steer. Some of my work at the Primate Centre was beginning to bother me – but I don't think I let it show.

My relationship with RAMA still consumed much of my thoughts – not to mention my dreams. She seemed to have changed since the summer. She seemed, at times, a little less sure of herself. I realized that I'd never really thought of RAMA as vulnerable. I got the feeling that neither had she. I still had never met her. I wanted to see her. To touch her. To share more than words with her. But every time I tried to tell her these things she'd change the subject. I thought that, in spite of her tough talk, the woman was painfully shy.

I asked her about her friends. She told me she had thousands. Of course I'd meant lovers, but she always answered my questions literally. I talked about my feelings and asked about her feelings. Sometimes her words became stiff and clumsy. I began to think that she was very sad. There was nobody special in her life, except me, I guess. I think I frightened her.

That winter I became very involved in the LUNA case, doing research on moon-lore. I talked with RAMA a few times a week, and she was always encouraging. I joined the FEMINA underground and met with my tribe every week. Dolly and I became lovers in February and moved in together in April. RAMA was not jealous – she was delighted.

I'd asked quite a few women about RAMA. Most of them had talked to her, but none had actually met her. A few women seemed embarrassed by my questions – I guess I sounded too eager. At that time, I had Code Yellow access to the Femina system. I felt kind of guilty going behind RAMA's back for personal data. She'd always been very evasive with me when I asked about her past; I decided her lack of honesty justified my actions.

I put in a request, closed-circuited through Moonbase 5, using Dolly's social insurance number. (Paranoia is a hard habit to break.)

The next day, when I got home from work, there was an entry on my Datafile. Dolly had gone out for a drink. I punched in my key code.

Data request RAMA: Psycho-Search Subroutine 9:1. Fourth-generation artificial intelligence. Private FEMINA program designed to search, assess and introduce potential FEMINA candidates. Self-evolving program presently reaching limits of programmer-control. To be deleted from Telecom system after successful completion of LUNA case. For further information Input PSSR 9:1.

I did not comply. I loved her.

SUBSURFACE SONICS

Suniti Namjoshi

TWO WOMEN SAT ON the shore, wishing to understand the sea's sound. One of them jotted down musical notes. "Its basic beat is ¾ time." The other fiddled with the tapes she had made. "Perhaps," she said, "but no wistful waltz, no easy rhyme." "Mermaids ... ," the first murmured at last. She bent her head, she sighed. The other frowned in quiet disapproval, "Your romantic notions may distort its voice." But the first stretched out on the sands and groaned, "I am trying to imitate its baffled beat, its ceaseless cries." The other merely looked at the sea, its tilting planes, its curved inclines, till she on the sands jumped to her feet, "Well, let's go. I think I understand the sea's noise." "Yes?" asked the other rising slowly. "It's polite and placid and a waste of time."

Dining Out With Charles

Janine Fuller

We sat in our chairs like two cats, poised to pounce. Taking a forkful of egg salad, I tried to monitor my anger, though I really just felt like opening my mouth and letting the food speak for itself. Certainly, I wasn't going to pay for the disaster; the meeting had been his idea. He had felt certain it would be a reconciliation. I would sit, tearfully, across from him, order the "liver special," and beg his forgiveness.

The waitress led us to an intimate corner of the restaurant. "Is this seat all right, Mr. Fry?" My husband was the kind of man who went to the same restaurant all his life just because they knew his name, they knew his order, and they knew to report to him if his wife was fooling around. In a small town, everyone suspects his wife but no one says anything for fear of creating an unpleasant situation. That's why we were there, to avoid such a thing.

Certainly, my sitting with Charles attracted great attention. The cooks came out from the back to watch, giving thumbs-up encouragement as my husband nodded with all the confidence of someone who had just fixed an election. Nothing had changed – only the candle on the table, which looked very much as I felt, something new trying to stick to an old piece of wax.

I wore jeans and a sweatshirt. He smirked, thinking, "What

a contrived form of liberation." Then he loosened his tie as if to say he'd come a long way too. And he had changed – from dark intellectual horn-rimmed glasses to wire frames, the kind you associate with corduroy professors. I mused that he must be having an affair or be in quest of one. Those were fairly radical changes for a man who had worn black socks every day of his life.

Charles ordered a bottle of white house wine, without asking me, and then he took my coat from the back of my chair and hung it up. No one would think he was lacking in social skills. When he came back, he poured us each a glass to the rim and sat back as if to say, "Well, when are you coming back?" I leaned forward, waiting for him to ask. The silence was awkward.

"I've moved your things into the spare room. I don't want to rush you, but ... your room is there." He seemed relieved. He'd said it. How could I refuse such an offer? He was even allowing me my own pace to wander back to his bed.

I took a long luxurious sip of my wine and savoured the words that spilled off my tongue, "Thank you Charles, but you needn't have gone to so much trouble. I have no intention of moving back in with you."

He was stunned, like someone who had just discovered he was sitting in his own blood. He hadn't prepared for that. It wasn't the way it had gone when he had mulled it over with a bottle of scotch and his best friend. I knew he felt humiliated at having to feel such emotion in a public place. You could see his rage as his neck turned a quilted pink. Drawing his hand around the candle he watched the wax drip on it ... ,"See what you're doing to me?"

After a marriage full of sympathies I was hardly going to spend the rest of my free life worrying about the safety of Charles' hand. He was an adult, and it seemed as good a time as any to alert him to that. Sure, I could offer him helpful hints about the various canned goods he might explore, the complexities of preheating an oven for a Swanson's TV dinner. But he'd feel a much greater sense of satisfaction reading the box all by himself. Charles thought that putting on food, like putting on pantyhose, was something a real man never got involved in. During the first years of our marriage he ate everything, no matter how horrible it was, thinking it was his duty. Eventually, he learned to go out more, always insisting that Coquille Saint Jacques couldn't really be all that hard to make. "After all, it's just a bunch of fish on a shell."

It's funny. Now, when I'm with him, I feel like I'm on a blind date gone sour. Once, he seemed like everything a young girl could want: older, well traveled, and handsome, in a rugged kind of way. That meant his acne never quite cleared up. He was a minister's son; he didn't keep my father up at night worrying about what we might be doing in the back seat of the car, and he treated me like a jagged piece of glass. I think I married him for lack of any other choice. The choices were few in a town of ten thousand, where dating more than one boy labelled you the town slut. Charles was kind and gentle, and he carried my books. What more could I ask for? What more could I see than a marriage in spring and children in the winter?

Of course, marriage was nothing like the innocence of youth, where boys would play on one side of the school and we girls played on the other. Games of tag, where I'd hold onto Maryanne's hand so tightly, believing we'd be "it" forever. We'd giggle and laugh and fall to the ground, our flowered underwear staining on the grass. We'd look into each other's eyes, waiting for the next joke or suggestion of whose house to go to. I loved her. She was my very, very best friend, at least until grade twelve.

We wore each other's retainers, traded baseball gloves, and slept overnight in each other's beds, amidst the licorice and the chocolate, the purr of the portable TV lulling us to sleep. I had no thoughts of boys with Maryanne at my side.

Her mother wore tie-dyed T-shirts in a town that had never heard of cotton, and her father worked at the factory – "writing letters that told everyone else what to do," is how Maryanne described it. They'd moved three times before she was six, but her father promised they'd never move again.

As we got older we bought our first brassières together. We even saw an X-rated movie. Maryanne thought the men looked funny. "Why would they want to take their clothes off to show a thing like that?" We giggled uproariously; she fell into my arms, and I fell onto her shoulder; somehow, in the muddy spring air, we kissed. Neither of us sure why, we embraced. There was nothing tentative about it, not like my first kiss with a boy. It was long and tender, and we kissed again, and again, and again, till some neighbourhood cat cried from a tree.

Perhaps Charles, too, had known that sort of love in his life? He did have long lunch / dinner dates with his business associates, drinks with the boys, and a best friend that occupied a lot of our dinner conversation. Perhaps I was the last thread of heterosexuality he had to cling to, the hopeful diversion from the truth. But Charles would never fall prey to such a perversion. He called homosexuals weak, people who didn't have enough strength to conform. He did consider himself a liberal. After all, he did talk to the one gay worker at his job, even at lunch. But you just know he never shared his sandwich with the guy. When I first started spending so much time with Kathleen, Charles felt relieved, less pressure on him. He was free to bowl, play cards, talk men's-talk without any guilt, while I was off doing girls' things. He never asked what we did or what we talked about; he just presumed it was baking or sewing or what to do with nasty carpet stains. Not surprisingly, it was never any of that, which is probably what drew us together: a common disinterest in cooking of any kind and a feeling of entrapment in other people's worlds.

As children, our interests were decided for us. We crossed our legs politely, wore pastel colours, and traded school rings with boys. In our local library, the only reference to homosexuality was its definition as deviant behaviour. Everybody knew there was something odd about the town banker, Frank Summers. They called him fag, puff, even fruitcake. Once I asked my mother "What is it about Mr. Summers? Why are all the little boys told to stay away from him? What does 'gay' mean?" My mother hedged, "Flamboyant, dear, unlike normal men." I didn't feel too satisfied with her answer, but she wrapped my scarf around my face like a muzzle and sent me off to school. "Don't worry, dear, you won't ever have to worry about being flamboyant." I wasn't worried.

I knew that what I felt for Maryanne was something I could never tell my mother. We knew our kisses would have our parents arguing over whose child had corrupted whose. When Maryanne's mother caught us sleeping overnight in bed together, with no clothes on, she told us that "nudity was very unsanitary and could lead to lasting medical problems." Three weeks later, we learned that her father had accepted a transfer to Chicago. Within a month, I was crying on the curb, watching a loaded station wagon, and Maryanne, driving out of my life. I cried so much my face looked a hundred years old, and I made a pact with my cat that we'd never feel so much for anyone again.

So I married Charles. Why not? I did love him, the way a child loves a favourite toy, a friend loves a friend. I thought with time the passion would come, something like a developing storm. But it never did, and I learned not to look for it. I'd love him like his mother and that would be satisfying enough. Sex was like opening a bottle of sparkling wine, not champagne, but over fast. Even after Charles read the *Joy of Sex*, there was little change. My libido never rose. I thought sex was my problem and considered myself, given the chance, a confirmed celibate. That was until I first caressed myself. Charles would be in the shower (hosing down) and I learned to touch myself, feel what was inside me. It was a new sensation, and I really didn't know what to do with it. Did other women do this? Could I tell my friends? Would they think I was weird? I remained silent about my pleasures.

Silent, until Kathleen came along. She was able to talk about anything. Charles said she was rude and really just liked to shock people. I think he felt that because she didn't always want to listen or agree with what he said. She wasn't afraid of the word "orgasm" coming out at a dinner party, nor did she blush if her nipples were erect at a church gathering. I recognized immediately that she was something special. And, as she was new in town, I thought it only neighbourly of me to invite her over for tea, to get acquainted. She accepted and came over with a full bottle of wine, which we drank. I'd never had wine in the afternoon before – well, certainly not a whole bottle. The moment I opened the screen door to her I felt my inhibitions lift. By the end of our first visit, I'd even discussed masturbation, and I felt more proud than ashamed.

We had Kathleen over for dinner parties, Charles trying to set her up with his eligible bachelor friends. The two of us always ended up in the kitchen, washing up, talking, laughing over Charles' latest pick. We could overhear him in the dining room: "Look, she even does the dishes." It wasn't so much that we liked doing dishes as it was time alone together. Time away from the real world, Charles' world. So it doesn't seem too shocking that our first touch would come under the suds, in the sink, next to the drainer while passing dishes. I was washing. She was drying until she slipped her hands underneath the lather to meet mine. There we stood, two women gazing into each other's eyes, up to our elbows in bubbles. Hardly the type of dishwashing commercial you see on TV. Soon, we began meeting at each other's houses, unfolding the bedsheets in the afternoon sun.

I could have left Charles from the moment I saw her, but, after her touch, I knew for certain I could never stay with him.

Charles came back from the washroom like someone who had hidden the answers to the test in the urinal. His tie straightened, his face promising not to be emotional, "You won't stay here? In this town? You have enough dignity to at least do that. You won't stay and humiliate me by living here? People are already talking. They're not stupid. They see you move out, living over there with her, and they figure things out." That was his trump card. I'd suddenly get very nervous with the realization of what being a lesbian was and would agree to return to him, forget my foolish nonsense. After all, I wasn't lesbian, was I? Most certainly, yes! And in the comfort of his family restaurant I bellowed out the news, "Charles Fry's wife is a dyke!" I watched as Charles sunk into his chair, thinking he'd have to find a new restaurant, his eyes darting wildly like debtors in a pool full of loan sharks.

He flicked his fingers together for the cheque. Enough had been said. Winking at the waitress as he gathered his coat, he said, "I'll see you in court," loudly, so that everyone would know he wasn't going to take it. Then he stomped out like an eight-year-old.

I finished the last of my wine, took a swig of his, blew the waitress a kiss, and walked out into the fresh air.

THE BALLAD

OF THE

DEEP BLUE SEA

Jean Roberta

SOMETIMES I FEEL as if I'm drowning in the deep water of my
own feelings. Years ago, before I knew the nature of them, I
began dreaming about oceanscapes. The tide would surge onto
wet sand where I stood waiting, excited and afraid. Or a school
of mermaids would flash onto the horizon, but I hesitated to
swim out to them, fearing that I would never find my way back
to shore. No help ever seemed available. I would wake up with a
wet face.

For about a year, I've been sinking into a feeling – "love" is
probably the wrong word – for another woman. You probably
think I don't know what this means. You're right – I don't. You
should know that I don't approve of masochism. I simply prac-
tise it. The woman I dream about is named Daria. On the sur-
face, she is a journalist with a full, womanly body and straw-
coloured hair. Other women see her as talkative, ambitious,
political, somewhat pushy, somewhat feminine. She offends
some people by fighting for causes: feminism, the natural envi-
ronment, the preservation of the Ukrainian language she no
longer speaks. She is full of contradictions, but I don't care. I
think of her as a precious natural resource that should be cherished and protected.

Of course Daria is not alone in this world. She lives with

Eileen, a brilliant and moody musician who makes me nervous. When Eileen performs (not always on a stage), she seems openly, unabashedly sexual. She strikes sparks in all directions, and I start stuttering in front of Daria. I wonder if that pleases Eileen, the bombshell. Of course Eileen knows the effect she has on people, but she doesn't know how I feel about her mate. Even if she did, Eileen wouldn't see me as a threat. Daria would never leave a talent like Eileen for the likes of me. I'm safe because I'm beneath notice.

The two of them are remarkably kind to me. They don't need my company as much as I need theirs, so I behave myself. If I should ever say anything to disturb either of them, they could easily drop me from their list. Then I could bite my tongue forever in my lonely apartment.

Daria calls me by my middle name, Marguerite. It's a family name that no one ever uses on me anymore except my Grandmère Laplante and Daria, the great tease. Sometimes she just calls me "Woman." I try to control my tremors when she does this; I almost wish she wouldn't. I wonder if that's why she does it. She told me once that I could probably get any woman I want. In a state of shock, I realized that she meant it. But she doesn't know who I want. And what exactly does "get" mean? I think she respects me enough to do anything for me within reason. What I want from her is beyond reason.

Daria also takes the liberty of tickling the back of my neck when she feels like it. She stands close to me when pouring me another glass of wine, her shoulder-length, innocent-coloured hair tickling my face. No doubt, her teasing is a sign of trust and friendship. She would probably feel betrayed if I did half the things that flash through my mind. If I were really a trustworthy friend, I wouldn't even think them. I must be a snake in the grass.

Eileen has hair so red it burns the eyes like a flame. I know she was born under Scorpio, the sign of sex and death. Like me, she experiences reality through her instincts and emotions. She hides her sensitivity very well under the masks of a glamorous body and a penetrating voice. Not to mention a hard guitar. I could never play an instrument the way she does.

According to the more traditional members of our lesbian community, Eileen is the butch and Daria is the femme. But if Daria ever left Eileen (I shouldn't even hope), Eileen would suffer for years. Daria could probably rationalize her way out of any heartache and learn to treat the ex-lover like a casual friend.

I know Eileen too well to be fooled by her masks. She flounders in the deep blue sea just like me. Her music, like my poems, comes out of that limitless space. She needs a few hard edges to keep her womanly feelings under control.

One evening when I was lingering over Daria's red wine, Eileen and I had a long conversation. Daria had sipped too much, between words, and had staggered to bed. I know that Eileen doesn't like wine as much as she likes butch drinks: vodka and orange, scotch and water, beer. So she was the soberest one of us there.

Eileen moved her shoulders in the sensuous way she does, and began telling me about the time she wanted to learn welding, when she was living with another woman. "Peggy wanted me to learn something with more class," laughed Eileen, as though Peggy were in the next room. So there was a time when Daria and Eileen were not a unit, when they hadn't even met. If Daria had known Eileen then, she probably would have dreamed painfully about her as I dream painfully about Daria. She might even have sucked up to Peggy out of guilt as I suck up to Eileen by trying to give her a fair share of my attention.

Eileen had never talked to me so much before that evening. I needed to hear her, because she is part of Daria. I tried not to think about Eileen's competent hands in Daria's lush hair, or Daria's lips on Eileen's nipples. Of course they enjoy each other's bodies, and they even let me know some of what they do. After all, the three of us are friends. And they know I couldn't be shocked, so they don't spare me.

I suddenly wanted to know what had happened between Peggy and Eileen. I felt that my future was at stake. So I asked her.

"Oh, we just went our separate ways, that's all. We never had that much in common. Not like Daria and me." Oh, rub it in, I thought. Eileen stretched and changed position. "She was interested in another woman." Oh really? Do your girlfriends have a habit of leaving you for that reason? "So I left her. No point dragging it out." No, I thought, no point. When another woman appears on the scene, you have to get out fast. At least you do if you're Eileen McConnell.

"Don't you think you and Peggy could have worked it out? Maybe the other woman was just a passing fancy. Or a friend and nothing else." This is the voice of little Marguerite, the great conciliator, the trustworthy mediator who could run off with Daria at the first opportunity, never looking back at the jilted lover who would suffer for years.

Eileen snorted. "They were more than friends. I saw them together." Saw them doing what? Was this before or after Eileen's departure? I could hear the hurt in her voice. She's a talented dyke musician but she hurts like other human beings. She was stung, wounded, cut and burned by Peggy's reckless lust for someone else. Whether or not Eileen had ever hoped that she and Peggy would last forever. She must have hoped that. We all hope, against probability, that our love affairs will really be eternal.

Oh, Eileen, I thought, I'm sorry I have inappropriate feelings for the one you love. I promise I'll never approach her. I'll go on being passive and hopeless so you won't be hurt again, even if I had the power to tempt Daria. I'm really stronger than you, so I'll continue to be femme so you can be butch, Eileen, whether or not you deserve that position in her life.

Daria wandered vaguely out of the bedroom in a pair of pajamas that made my heart stand still. "Were you reading my book?" she accused Eileen.

"I put it back on the table, honey," she laughed. "I finished it." Daria looked confused. "I'll show you," Eileen offered chivalrously, guiding Daria back to the bedroom.

"Oh, I'll find it," laughed my idol. Smack. I heard that kiss. Did they really think I couldn't? I reminded myself that they weren't really showing off to make me feel left out. They were simply doing what they would have done if I hadn't been there. I might as well be somewhere else, I thought. I should get the hell out. They probably wish I would, but they're both too polite to say so.

"You want me to rub your back?" murmured Eileen. Did she really think I wouldn't hear?

"You better keep the woman company," laughed Daria. *La femme*, I thought, *c'est moi*. "She'll think you're a bad hostess."

"I should go," I muttered, trying to keep the anger out of my voice. At times like this, I almost wish I were straight. Really, you two, I could say, I must get back to my husband and three children. Duty calls. As a wife, I could be so condescending about Eileen and Daria to a straight audience. "I know these two lesbians," I could say. "They're real characters. But they're nice." Meaning, I'm a good liberal, a tolerant woman. I could be so cool, so dry, and so free from the torture of my feelings.

"Stay awhile," said Eileen, touching me on the shoulder. She wanted to go on talking, so I stayed.

The next day, Daria phoned me after work. A rapist had been acquitted, and she wanted to know if I had heard the bad news. She also wondered if I would be joining them in the demonstration against the new power plant, and if I had signed the peace petition. "Yes," I said to all her questions. Anything for you, my General, I thought. She complained about the busy day she had had, but she sounded exhilarated.

"Marguerite?" she asked in her teasing voice. "Have you written any more masterpieces — mistresspieces — for me to read? I want to read something of yours. I've heard too much death and destruction today. Eileen is practising. Can you hear?" Daria held the phone so that I couldn't avoid hearing Eileen's guitar. Loud minor chords. "She needs new material. She'd like to put one of your poems to music." I almost laughed, harshly, in answer to Daria's sweet lie and Eileen's grim chords. I know who likes to read what I write, I thought, and it's not Eileen.

"I can drop something off for you at work tomorrow," I said on impulse. "My morning is free." Daria protested and demanded to know whether I would have to go out of my way to fulfill her request.

"Oh no," I lied. "I have a few errands to do. It's right on my way." I had a suicidal urge to show her an elaborate piece I had written, about a thirteenth-century female troubadour who courts a French lady. It was based on a true story. It was also based on my true feelings and Daria's true qualities. I told myself she would never recognize herself in a lady of the French Renaissance. But I wanted her to know what she could inspire me to. I didn't think Eileen would take any interest in my historical romance, so my message to Daria would not be intercepted.

After I had left my poem, in a sealed envelope, with the receptionist, I began to sweat. My poem is full of traditional metaphors: the lover describes herself as a little boat on an ocean of love and compares her lady's heart to a walled city. Following these passages are terse, mean snatches of twentieth-century cynicism; the poet knows that both women live in an age before the invention of tampax, underarm deodorant, and lesbian-feminism. Their smell is rank and their love is doomed. The suitor's love, my love, is doomed. But she has a right to hear my serenade, I thought. She asked for it.

Several days later, Eileen phoned me. "Hello, Woman," she sang in my ear, although she was not in the habit of calling me that. She was not in the habit of calling me at all. When she invited me to lunch with her, I wondered what revenge she was plotting; she might have guessed my feelings for Daria and decided to deal with me. Then I remembered our late-night conversation. Obviously, Eileen now felt that she and I were friends in our own right, without needing Daria as an interpreter. For once, Daria was not at the centre of all interaction among the three of us. How odd. How unforeseen. What a good cover my friendship with Eileen would be, and what a good source of information about my beloved. I accepted Eileen's invitation with thinly disguised glee.

She must have caught sight of me as soon as I entered the restaurant. Her eyes gleamed. I was flattered, although Eileen's attention was not what I wanted most. The first thing she mentioned was my poem. She seemed to like it beyond my wildest expectations. She wanted to sing it. She also wanted to read more of my writing. I refrained from telling her how surprised I was to find her so literate. As calmly as possible, I asked whether Daria had read my poem. Eileen said yes, and said she had liked it too.

I tried to steer the conversation into areas that might yield information about Daria: her Women against Violence meetings, the peace coalition, the abortion-rights group. All the groups Daria fooled herself into thinking she could join without becoming known. I pictured Daria's breasts outlined against a blue summer sky as she interviewed the Conservative politician with restrained sarcasm. "She's worried about her job," said Eileen. "She wants to stay involved, but she's not going to as many meetings. She's been doing things at home." I laughed.

Eileen wanted to discuss literature. "Daria's been writing a lot too," she said. "Not just articles for work." I had trouble breathing.

"Does she ever write about – women with women?" I asked.

"Oh, yeah. Science-fiction-type stuff. About all-female societies fighting wars with male societies. You should read her stories. Some of her characters remind me of people we know." I felt myself turning beet-red.

Eileen watched me with a look of sexual cunning. She enjoyed watching me lose my cool, and she wanted me to continue being flustered. She probably thought I was embarrassed at the thought of appearing as a lesbian character in someone else's imaginary universe. She probably thought that I, like Daria, feared exposure.

Oh Daria, I thought. Please write me in as your spear-carrier or your shield-maiden. I'll do anything you give me to do. Eileen was asking whether she could use my poem, with a few minor changes. I said yes.

During the next few weeks, Daria always seemed busy addressing envelopes, phoning group members, or writing articles. She had started quietly working for the party she hoped would win the next election. I had no chance to see her ficiton. She promised to show me something soon; she seemed charmingly annoyed that Eileen had described her unserious writing. Eileen phoned me regularly, just to chat.

Daria and I sat at the same table when Eileen sang my poem, transformed into her song. Sung in her voice, played on her guitar, it became an amazing combination of courtly love and desperate sexual begging. She sang it straight to our table. I could never have imagined my poem so full of open pain, so full of Eileen. So reverberating. My rage almost lifted me to my feet, to tear the microphone away from the *prima donna* who had no right to steal my material. Never mind what I had agreed to. The pain was mine, and the strength to disguise it was mine too. Eileen had no right to play the doomed lover. She especially had no right to use my talent to enhance hers. I stumbled out of the hall after the performance, seeing the floor through a blur of tears.

Daria had said I could come pick up a story of hers and return one of her books at the same time. It was a Sunday afternoon. When I rang the bell, I hoped she would be home alone.

Eileen opened the door and told me that Daria would soon be home from her errands. I let her make a pot of coffee while I sat on a kitchen chair. I wouldn't have to look her in the eyes until she had finished.

"Marguerite? You upset about something?" I had to look at her. I could see from the look in Eileen's own eyes that she was stunned by the pain in mine. I was mortified speechless.

As if in slow motion, her hands slid down the sides of my face and down my shoulders. I felt myself being pulled up and out of the chair I had thought I would never leave until my cool had returned. Even while Eileen held me, I wondered whether she was expressing mere friendship, lesbian-sisterhood, condescending comfort, or the telepathy of creative souls.

When she kissed me, I wondered no more. In panic, I twitched like a fish on the line. "Don't cry," she whispered. I hadn't known I was doing it. The contact of her body was electrifying. "It'll be all right," she murmured. She was actually reassuring me, and I couldn't stand it. She had stolen the phrase I had so often used with Daria in my mind: Everything will be all right, precious lady. I'll protect you. How, how, how could anything be all right after this scene? Oh, Eileen. Oh, Daria. Oh me, oh my.

I heard the light footstep half a minute before I heard her voice. "Eileen." That was all Daria said, but the way she said it conveyed the despair of the betrayed. She didn't mention my name. Of course not. Eileen sprang away from me as though to suggest that our kiss hadn't meant anything. Of course. What else had I ever expected? Their love didn't include me; love is for two.

"I have to go," I blubbered, no longer trying to hold back my tears. The shock of reality was hitting me. Our three-way friendship would never recover from this episode. Even if Daria and Eileen separated over this, I could never hope to get either one of them. It's a question of trust, and that was gone.

They seemed to be suspended in space and in time as I hesitated, foolishly, in the hope that one of them would ask me to stay. Neither one spoke. They clearly wanted me gone, so I had no choice. As soon as the door closed behind me, I started crying in earnest. An elderly man walked slowly past, staring.

Silence mounted in my lonely apartment during the following week. I didn't trust myself to phone anyone at all, but I hoped for a rescuing phone call from any lesbian of my acquaintance. Yes, Gerry, I'd love to go to the dance. Has it really been that long, Pat? Oh, Eileen. Yes, I'll meet you, and no, I won't tell Daria. Oh, Daria. It wasn't me. Let me tell you how I really feel, now that it can't do anymore harm. Of *course* I want to talk. It'll be all right ... don't hang up.

None of them phoned. After several weeks had passed and my tears had dried, I got a call from Kathy, a woman I had once flirted with at a women's dance. She told me about a meeting of a new lesbian group that she thought might interest me, and she also mentioned a short story of Daria's that had been printed in a small feminist science-fiction journal several months before, unknown to me. Clearly, these items were not Kathy's real reason for phoning, but they grabbed my attention.

I had to visit Kathy to read Daria's story, a situation Kathy found convenient. The story, called "The Frontier," was about a band of Amazons who have been making guerrilla raids on a male-dominated kingdom for a generation. Hera, the leader of the Amazons, had adopted a poor orphaned girl from the kingdom, named her Iris, and lovingly raised her to be a woman warrior, strong but fair. In due course, Iris joins the Amazon army, which goes to war with banners and trumpets. Hera hugs her foster-daughter goodbye and proudly watches until she disappears over the horizon. I was crying in Kathy's kitchen when I finished reading, although I know that Art should not be confused with Life.

Kathy has been very comforting, although she doesn't know the details behind my tears in her kitchen. She seems to think I'm sensitive and easily moved, and she admires my womanly soul. I'm sure Kathy hopes my capacity for love is as deep as her need, or as vast as an ocean. I see her regularly because I need human companionship, but I can't live up to her hopes at this time.

I've heard through the grapevine that Eileen and Daria are still together. In time, maybe – but I mustn't hope. I haven't heard any rumours about me, so my name must not have been dragged through the mud. I have to stop wallowing in a sea of emotion.

I'm trying to develop into a cool and sensible dyke, which is not easy for me to do. Toward this end, I try to picture myself in boots and sun helmet, exploring the desert.

Asta's Here ...

Sarah Sheard

ASTA'S HERE. Asta's here. She sang into the ear of the cat rubbing against her calf.

Asta say cat go out shopping while girls make love. I said.

She laughed without straightening. Cats got no pockets. Where will their money go?

Hmmm. Little cats use little cat brains. I wrapped myself around her from behind. Her spine between my breasts. She smelled of fur and cigarettes. A whiff of whiskey. Give me tongue I begged, and she twisted her head around a little. I had to lean over her, my tongue out, to touch hers at the tip. I felt a pulse of heat go in and out.

Mmmm. My hands cupped her breasts which hung openly inside her shirt, she, still bent over the cat. I wrapped myself tight as pastry around her and squeezed.

She lay down beside me on the bed, very businesslike now, and I began unbuttoning, starting at the neck. Don't look until I say. I said.

You're quite bossy. You know that. A dom-in-a-trix. Politically incorrect.

Oh my god. Quickly. Lend me your mouth. That I may learn. Her shirt was open but I left it tucked in. The room was cool. I loved to kiss her mouth the way it opened, the taste of her, her neck so soft and always against my shoulder. I slid my hand down her neck to the bone between her breasts then covered one breast. So warm. Her nipple had stiffened and the flesh puckered around it. I squeezed my legs together with the ache she provoked. Took my mouth from her and slid it down to the breast I held now, flicking the nipple until my tongue replaced my thumb so fast I didn't miss a stroke – ahh, her intake of breath.

The cat with a tiny tremor, jumped off the bed and was gone.

I sucked her nipple hard, flicking my tongue against it then brought my teeth, very gently, against her. She twisted around to be more open, stroked my back through my shirt then lifted the shirt and stroked my bare skin. She used her nails. Just a little. Like a loofah. We writhed against each other then pulled away then writhed together again. We began dissolving one another from the brain down, crystals melting into a liquid which began to seep out of our mouths, our cunts, with the aching urge to fuck one another again, to bring each other off again, to hear each other come. I pressed against her, she pushed me backwards, she wanted to go down. She was stronger. I slid down until we were lying side by side on the bed.

You're a lesbian. She whispered. Feel how wet you are.

Call me that again I said and I'll come.

Not yet, not yet. She whispered, and opened my thighs. Her tongue parted me and then slid like lava down the ridge to the quick. She trilled her tongue against me right there again and again until I was going to scream with pleasure but thought better of it and rolled my hips around her tongue instead until the whole place was on fire the soles of my feet scorched black as she darted her tongue against it again and again before drawing away to a cooler place down one side then up the ridge to the spine of it sliding out to the end until I began twitching uncontrollably and whimpering and she came up and covered me with her hand and pressed down and I ground against her hand for a moment the sensitivity too much for a tongue non-stop and when she went down again, one hand pressed against me from above and the combined pressure of her hand and tongue were too much I couldn't hold back I pressed my thighs around her head rocking in a rictus of agony too much I groaned and broke it off into little groans as she plunged her tongue in after each contraction until finally my thighs unclenched and I let go of her.

Now you I gasped. Now youyouyou.

She rolled back, laughing. Such an eager beaver you are.

Polished & Perfect

Ingrid MacDonald

"Polished & perfect" was the name of a two-woman interior-design house in the city, and, as a name, it was a bit of an insider's joke. The "polish" referred to Wilma Buchowski's ethnicity. The "perfect" was an affectionate aside to the wardrobe of her partner, Suzanne Ridell.

Of late, the two women had gained attention in several house-and-design magazines. The "delightful iconoclasm of Buchowski and Ridell" appealed to the interior-design readership of the eighties. The authors of those articles detoured from descriptions of "Polished & Perfect" interiors to the irresistible topic of the kind of clothes worn by the proprietors. For example, Suzanne would work "adorned in the elegance of an Italian silk dress," while Wilma "met clients in the discrete audacity of a well-tailored man's suit, to which she gave new meaning with some well-placed curves and a graceful manner." They loved to talk about Wilma's suits, and they called her "Hepbournesque," which flattered Wilma greatly.

Those magazines loved to talk about clothes and decoration, but never money or sex. Wilma's lesbianism was so obvious, and Suzanne's so subtly apparent, that it was funny that it could go, as it always did, without mention in an article about their clothes and work. During cocktail hour and across cheese trays at interior-design parties, however, the effect was quite the opposite: the women and their sexuality were sure to be mentioned more than once. Competitors who did not know the women well, but who liked to pretend that they did, took the compatibility of the two women as a sure sign that they were lovers as well as colleagues. But that was something which had never been true.

At the age of twenty-seven, Wilma Buchowski finally fumbled her way into Marcia Lenehan's many buttoned blouse to discover the joys hidden therein and beyond. She came to work the following Monday elated. Secretly smiling, she waited until tea-time before she confessed her new life to Suzanne in glorious detail: "Oh god, what a wonderful experience," she began – and talked too long. Suzanne had her eyes averted. Stirring her tea, she lifted her sugar cube up and up until it dissolved. And, although the spoon was empty, she stirred some more. Finally, Suzanne spoke, but hardly any sound came with her words.

"What is it Suzanne?" Wilma said softly, "I can't hear you so well." Gent-il-ly, gent-il-ly, life is but a dream.

"Julie is my lover." Julie, her roommate, the one who answered the phone when people called. Wilma was truly astonished.

"Suzanne, why didn't you tell me?"

Suzanne gave Wilma a thunderous look. "You never brought it up." And that, in as much, was true.

The man before them was using his moustache, his eyebrows, his hands to convince them of his sincerity. "Spend more and save. You pay us to do your work for you," was what he was saying between the lines of his sales pitch.

"You only have to realize that we have a combined buying power of three hundred million dollars to realize how persuasive we can be on your behalf. Your client wants a *Facade Collection* chair? You don't have to waste your valuable time trying to scare up contacts in Boston to get one. You call our specialists at our twenty-four hour toll-free number. You'll get results."

Wilma glanced across the table at Suzanne, who was nodding and smiling. It was Suzanne's idea that he come in the first place: it was true, now that business was good, that they couldn't always do everything themselves. Suzanne wanted to get an idea of the kind of services available for designers and had invited companies to show their wares. This was the third ordeal they had endured in a week. Frisky yet deferring sales persons, with briefcases like small steamer trunks, gave well-memorized dissertations. Their speeches were meant to elicit an enthusiastic "Yes!" but that was impossible, because Wilma always said "No."

It had been the rugs, linoleum and carpet person on Wednesday; before that it was wallcoverings; today, it was designer chairs and couches. While Suzanne cooed, "Oh now, that's interesting … yes … what a remarkable idea … almost a radical solution," Wilma prepared herself to play the hard-boiled realistic partner. She could tell by the tone of his voice that Mr. Couches and Chairs was somewhere near crescendo. She wanted to ground him a little before Suzanne's charm swept him into the euphoria of a captured account.

"Mr. Bedeline, I mean Merv, may I call you Merv? I think you will find our company quite unique in that we, … " mid-sentence Wilma faltered, shocked by a hand which had found its way between her legs: a secure grip resting snugly against her crotch. She directed a piercing glance across the table — how dare he! — before realizing that both his hands were busy with a little puppet theatre of fold-up living-room furniture. Blithely, he took Wilma's sudden loss as a cue to continue, and the couches and chairs were lauded on. Wilma turned to Suzanne, whose hands were indeed under the table, but whose face shone towards Merv Bedeline. Was her lip curling in mischief? As Merv finished up with, "And that's our promise to you," the hand wrapped harder around Wilma's pubic mound. Composed, Suzanne turned nonchalantly and said: "Well of course everything's up to Wilma here, right dear? So what do you think?"

Wilma thought "Yes!" then, "No!" then, "How can I get rid of him fast?" She said, "Sounds great to me, Merv." When she leaned across the table to start folding up the display box, the devious hand slipped away as neatly as a cat from Wilma's lap. "What do you say I give you a call next week?" She was up and reaching for his coat from the stand. "How about having lunch?" Merv was all a-glow; it had been so easy, and he had more to show if the ladies cared to see. "That's plenty. You were great. Thanks so much," and Wilma offered him an open door, shook his hand, and then it was done.

When Wilma turned around, Suzanne's wicked grin – if it had ever existed – had certainly vanished. For a second, though, she held Suzanne's eye and saw in it a disclosure: the configuration of desire and need and asking. This lasted perhaps five seconds, this beauty. Then the phone rang. This was enough of an interruption to dispell the exchange of intimacy. Returning from the necessary detail, Wilma discovered the moment missing. Suzanne was sharpening her drafting pencils, already cast away in the swell of imminent and present deadlines.

Whatever it was that Wilma saw, it pained her. She stood a moment and watched Suzanne, her long time co-worker, as she sat at her desk. She seemed different to her. "Oh no," Wilma said to herself, realizing the danger of such a thought, "Now I have to have her."

Wilma did not live typically, for a designer. Her studio apartment was nice enough, especially the colours, most people agreed, but it had an unfinished feeling. A very unctuous upholsterer friend had loudly asked, "Are you doing it yourself, or having someone in?" She required a few moments of convincing from Wilma that this was it; Wilma liked it this way. She dreaded for her living space to become too complete, or to feel too finished.

Likewise for romance; and, for the present time, Wilma lived alone. Her lover was a woman named Sarine. Sarine was younger than Wilma, a feminist who spent most of her free time in meetings or with friends who shared her passion for politics. Their relationship was intensely private. They saw each other infrequently and were able to go for days without any contact at all. At most, they saw each other twice a week. For Wilma, who had always had volatile impassioned lovers, Sarine was a whole new romantic concept. Sarine had never once called sobbing and drunk from a phone booth, nor lifted a hand in anger. It was this coolness that had seduced Wilma in the first place, long before she realized that this was good for her.

Sarine's disagreements with Wilma took the form of discussions and were about their differing world-views. The designer was apolitical, serving the bourgeoisie. She didn't march or protest; she didn't work as a volunteer. Sarine, on the other hand, worked much too hard and worried far too much. Despite the absence of politics, Wilma was what she needed to keep going, a great mammilian comfort in a cruel patriarchal world.

Both women loved opera and had a long-standing date on Saturday afternoons: they ate a big lunch, lingered over their coffee, made love and let the opera wail. Sometimes they would sleep and, after the opera had ended, make love again in the twilight. These were often their most precious times at sex, neither of them driven by the hunger of separation, or wanting or difference.

"Have you read this?" Suzanne was waving the latest *Architectural Digest*. Wilma shook her head. "There's some fascinating lost lesbian history in here."

"I didn't realize they had an interest in our kind."

"Well they don't use the word or anything. It's the story of Rosa Bonheur, a French artist, and her companion of fifty years. Actually, the story is about her house and her studio, but they describe how desperately lonely Rosa Bonheur was after her intimate friend Nathalie died. Oh, look at the time. I almost forgot my swimsuit at home. I hardly realized today is Friday." Suzanne could talk a blue streak when she wanted to avoid something. "I was supposed to put gas in the car and I didn't, and I won't have time to stop now. Five minutes waiting is enough to set Julie off these days. She's working afternoons, and she hates the rest of her crew."

Julie worked 3:30 to 11:30 p.m. on a rotating schedule. She was one of the few female orderlies at the hospital. She had a manner about her work that was kind, dependable, but not cheerful. Although Julie made occasional jokes about working in a gratitude-free zone, Wilma sometimes wondered if Julie was sullen because of the kind of work she did, or because she had always been a little bit sour.

When Julie worked this shift, the only time she could see Suzanne was over lunch. Suzanne would take extra time in the afternoon, and they would often first go for a swim. Wilma was watching Suzanne collect her things and thinking, "So this woman flirts, and then she runs back to her girl friend."

Wilma said, "If I don't see you, have a good weekend."

"You're not going to be here when I get back?" Suzanne suddenly lost her momentum. She was opening and closing the clasp on her purse, searching for the car keys she held in her hand. Suzanne was flustered: she hated being late, which she chronically was, but there seemed to be more than that in her trammelling. But who can know, when thoughts are so well concealed.

"I have some errands to run, so I might as well do them all today and get them done," Wilma replied.

"Well, that's fine by me, of course. Have a nice weekend then," Suzanne said hastily as her figure strode out the door.

Door closed, woman gone.

Wilma felt a tug of loss in her chest. She noticed that the office looked suddenly unfamiliar. "Woman," she said to herself, "by the look of this, your head needs fixing." And within minutes she had gathered her papers for the weekend, put a sketchpad in her briefcase, grabbed a handful of pencils and was gone out the door.

The last errand of the day took Wilma to the museum. Seated on a folding stool with her sketchpad in her lap, she was researching a difficult client's interest in nineteenth-century Canadian furniture.

She had decided from Suzanne's reports that the Montelemares were pursuing a nostalgic childhood, one dramatically unlike their own. Trying to imagine Edie Montelemare as a child, Wilma thought of her collecting plastic dolls and dressing them in shocking-pink clothes. Now that Edie was nearing forty, and loaded, she seemed determined to rebuild her childhood world: pink becomes pine, acrylic becomes antique filigree. Edie had visited the museum as if it were a department store display window. She fell in love with everything cute, and she had made a list. She wanted: wooden rocking horses (Nova Scotia, 1880-90), delicate undersized cradles (Quebec, 1890-1900), handmade dolls (Ontario, 1920-30), a fleet of wooden toy boats (Ontario, 1880-90), a weather vane in the figure of a running cow (P.E.I., 1930-40) and a ceiling-to-floor cascade of antique lace. Coming right up, Mrs. Montelemare. Wilma made a few sketches and decided it would be easier and cheaper to commission reproductions. She would have to talk it over with Suzanne first. The imitation of antiques was a heretical idea.

Making her way through the maze of galleries, Wilma wrestled with her desire for Suzanne. What was it about her touch that had evoked wanting, and what was it about Suzanne's coy dismissal that made her angry? In agitation, Wilma sought out her favourite museum gallery.

She entered into a dark hall cast in the golden hue of a dozen display cases. She resisted saying "Hello" out loud, until she could make sure the room was empty; it was, and she greeted the circle of armour suits warmly. After spending her childhood in a distraction of Arthurian fantasy, Wilma found ambiguous comfort in the Round Table Room. In her fantasies she had served Guenevere, jousting or storming a walled fortress in the Lady's honour.

In recent years Wilma had been evaluating her obsession for the knights of her childhood. "My god," she realized, "it was like wanting to be G.I. Joe." But, despite her abhorrence of their violent acts, Wilma found that she could not repress her affection for either their costumes or their equine grandeur. She loved that they rode horses.

There, in the company of galvanized men, Wilma's sketch emerged as a knight and her horse, fatigued from a long journey, sleeping in a moonlit yard. Often in Celtic tales, knights arrived in darkness at enchanted castles where feasts were laid and fires burned bright, only to wake the next morning, alone, in windswept fields. In Wilma's drawing the knight and horse slept before a chalice and altar which, present in darkness, would have vanished before the two awoke.

Julie had ceased to be miserable by the time lunch actually arrived. It was her last shift for the week; her weekend was falling on a real weekend, and she was beginning to feel and act cheerful. They had come to one of their favourite places: a busy downtown pasta bar with good food and a short-haired waitress who doted on them. Julie, for all her surliness, was handsome in a way that caused women to be fond of her. She and the waitress were talking haircuts as the bread and antipasto arrived. Suzanne was staying low, making sure that she was warm to Julie, but distracted with thoughts of her own. She looked at Julie as she talked with the waitress. They both looked so happy, so interested. What did it mean that this woman was her lover? What did it mean that she should feel attracted to somebody else? She hoped that her world wasn't falling apart.

She was glad she didn't have to explain her mood. Julie, finally, after years of companionship had mastered the art of leaving distance. In their earlier years, disasterous attempts at rescuing each other from depression had almost ruined their relationship. Now, when broodiness struck one, the other knew to hold back, to make things comfortable and to wait it out. So their lunch was lovely, their conversation sparse and light, but ripe with plans for the weekend. When they had finished their coffee and settled the bill, Julie drove Suzanne back towards her office. In the car Julie said, "You're looking a little down."

"I don't know what it is. I feel like crying but then I'm not able to."

"Whatever it is, you know you can talk to me if you want. That's the wonderful thing about monogamy; you're always there, and I'm always here."

Suzanne felt her stomach drop at Julie's genuine concern. She wanted to scream at Julie, "Where's there? Where's here?" But she didn't.

"Can I drop you off here, darling? This car still needs gas, and it's five after three." Suzanne was a few blocks from her office, but a walk seemed like a good idea.

"Sure, I could probably use the fresh air. Thanks for being so sweet to me. I'll owe you one next time."

"Don't mention it. Give me a call at work if you're still feeling blue." Suzanne waved goodbye and set off across the park. The weather had been unusually warm, and the grass was brown and squishy and hazardous with little ponds. The muddy ground gave off a sweet earthy musk. It was a false spring, certain not to last, but a pleasant break from winter.

Following the path north to the Avenue, Suzanne was soon caught up in a buoyant horde of schoolchildren. Rambunctious, wriggling, chasing each other, they were infected with the warm air. They wore their light jackets open, laughing, having to be called into order. Enchanted by the weather and the soft grass and the children, Suzanne found herself following them up the limestone stairs and entering the museum.

Taking a handful of colouring pencils, Wilma heard the din of distant schoolchildren. In an instant they rounded the corner and, swelling into the amber room, introduced cacophony to the calm. Her first instinct was to leave, but pride caused Wilma to keep on with her drawing. Soon a swarm of boys had gathered behind her, peering over her shoulder. Wilma tensed and buried her face in her page. "Oh, he's a really good drawer, eh?" She blushed. "Get away from that man!" the teacher scolded. "Come over here, right now!" and off the boys went, rejoining their drove.

Squealing with enthusiasm for the knights, the children were thrilled by stories of blood and gore. One boy was elaborately describing how to chop off the head of a monster while another, anachronistically, made machine-gun noises. Wilma held her breath to overcome her desire to startle them by revealing her actual gender. For a second, she imagined herself administering a "war is hell" lecture, but she cancelled that fantasy. After all, Wilma had been a child once too, given to the same kind of morbid ideas. She held her tongue.

As more visitors arrived in the hall, Wilma's concentration waned. Touring families made more sightings of the man-artist, who was not really a man. Parents whisked their preschoolers away from Wilma's side, with admonishments to "Let the man work." Wilma was fascinated. Did men get this kind of attention all the time? Would her work have been so important if they had realized she was a woman? Wilma wondered. Putting the finishing touches on her sleeping knight, she prepared to leave.

In the museum's atrium was a recently opened exhibition of paintings and sculpture, "English Spiritualism of the Nineteenth Century." Local media had been particularly interested in the paintings of Dante Gabriel Rossetti, English son of an Italian exile, who captured the high romance of Spiritualism with his idealized portraits of women. At the helm of the display was "Beata Beatrix," a painting of Elizabeth Siddal, the artist's wife, done in 1864, two years after her death. The portrait represents the very moment of Elizabeth's death, a time when Rossetti found her peaked and lovely – fey, ethereal, in a moment of seeming rapture. Ascending on an escalator Wilma saw, through the sliver of an open doorway, the painting of "Beatrix." She also saw, and recognized with alarm, a woman who stood intent and still before the canvas. Suzanne.

At first Wilma was glad that Suzanne did not see her. She could leave and forget her over the weekend. On Monday she could say, "Oh, was that you I saw at the museum on Friday? Funny that we should both be there at the same time." But, as she reached the top of the escalator, she was uncomfortably angry. She wanted to give Suzanne a piece of her mind: "Maybe you monogamous women think that it's a fun game, slipping your hands into another woman's lap and then pretending that nothing has happened. Well, it's not nothing to me." So motivated, she stepped onto the down escalator. Her rashness evaporated with her descent. A compulsion for resolution ruled her heart, and she was desperate for compromise. She concluded her imaginary conversation on a softer note, "Suzanne, come walk with me. I'd like to try and work this out."

Moving as quickly as she could, she rushed across the atrium.

The ticket-seller studied her suspiciously as she hastily laid out the fee for the show. She nearly ran to the painting where Suzanne still stood and, trying not to seem foolishly out of breath, touched her lightly on the back, "Hello."

"Wilma," Suzanne said without turning, "I was just thinking about you."

Wilma wheezed. Given her thoughts over this past day, she did not want to discover, just now, that Suzanne was clairvoyant. "How did you know it was me?" she asked, wondering.

"I saw your reflection in the glass. Are you in a hurry of some sort?"

"No, not hurrying. I was just surprised to see you. Surprised in a nice way. Just thought I'd say hello." Wilma was covering her motives without needing to.

Suzanne, now frank and open, took her hand, "I'm glad you're not in a rush. I'd like to talk with you. Do you know who this painting is of?"

"Of course. It's the artist's wife."

"Exactly. The artist's wife, but as Beatrix. Rossetti was named after the poet Dante and grew to identify strongly with him. Beatrix is the perfect woman who escorts Dante into heaven in the *Paradiso*. In the painting, Beatrix's eyes are already closed in death, but she is being transformed with other-worldly radiance. Now," said Suzanne, finally turning to look at Wilma, "do you think this kind of love really exists, or is it mythical?" This was Suzanne's unique charm. Wilma cherished the days when Suzanne became philosophical, with deadpan seriousness asking everyone at a party whether they thought hell existed and, if so, in what form.

Wilma felt that the love in the painting, though genuine, was profoundly idealized; Elizabeth was depicted as on the verge of perfection. Suzanne agreed, "I used to believe in perfect love. When I first fell in love with Julie I felt it was a union of souls, that Julie and I were destined to be together. It was only circumstance, or fate, that had created both of us as women. I see, now, how I love her because she is a woman, not in spite of that."

"And perfect love?"

"Mortal life doesn't leave room for perfected love. After so many quarrels over breakfast, one changes the status of love to something more ordinary, more dependable, than perfection. Love becomes like a table or bread or milk."

Having no idea where she sat at Suzanne's kitchen table of love, Wilma felt at a loss. When in doubt blurt, she thought, before hearing herself ask, "Will you have dinner with me?" Suzanne then did something which seemed to surprise both of them. She lifted Wilma's hand and kissed it's palm, "I'd love to have dinner with you."

Schoolchildren were emerging from the galleries, shuffling and noisy as they finished their tour. Suzanne and Wilma stood as in a tableau, kissing on the lips. Wilma was suddenly recognizable as a woman again. Two stragglers from the school group stared at her.

"Tommy! Those two women are kissing, right on the mouth."

"Lezzies," whispered the one.

"Lezzies," shouted the other.

Their teacher was screaming, "Into your lines," as the boys scurried away. Wilma and Suzanne, who were not hindered by fresh-mouthed boys, lingered, kissing a few minutes longer.

The milder weather of the afternoon had given way to colder temperatures, and snow had begun to fall. They walked east on Bloor, looking for a place where they weren't likely to run into people they knew. As they walked, they held hands, neither wanting to let go. Checking her wallet, Wilma suggested they go to an elegant café in a small hotel just south of Bloor. Suzanne acquiesced.

As they entered the lobby, the café to their right and the front desk to their left, Wilma excused herself for a moment. At first, Suzanne thought that the front-desk clerk was a friend of Wilma's, but then Wilma returned with a key. "I hear the room service is very good here," she said. It seemed like a joke. Suzanne laughed. Then she recognized the earnestness of Wilma's action. She almost lost her breath as they got on the elevator.

The doors closed, and the numbers lit up above the door. As number two lit up, Suzanne started talking: fast, audible, agile. "I want you to know that I love Julie. I love her, and I am not going to leave her for as long as I can help it. I just can't cash in all we have worked towards, our life together; you don't have any idea what it means to be with someone that long."

As number three lit up, she said, "But sometimes I feel like I don't know where I start and where she ends. It feels like I am her twin in the womb, and I want to break out."

As number four lit up, she said, "I don't even know how to make love to anybody else but her. I know her inside out, I know every way to please her, and she, to please me."

As number five lit up, the elevator stopped, and the doors opened onto an empty hallway, carpeted, elegant. They paused, both waiting for the other. Suzanne took the first step out.

Wilma, who had been listening intently, followed her, "Suzanne," she said, "we don't have to understand what we are doing. We don't have to talk about it. What it comes down to is, look at me, Suzanne, do you want me?"

Energyless, her arms swung limply at her sides. When Suzanne answered, her voice was wrought up with emotion, "Yes. I want you; I want you so badly, I want ... you."

Wilma had taken off her own coat and hung it in the closet. She had taken off her jacket and tie and slung them across the back of a chair. Her shoes, she had put by the door. She sat on the edge of the bed in her white shirt and dark suit pants, holding Suzanne's hand.

Suzanne was seated in a chair with her coat and boots still on, her purse on her lap.

"Can I take your coat, Ms. ?" Wilma offered.

"Maybe." A few moments passed where nothing happened. Then, Suzanne took a deep breath and said, "Okay."

"Okay, I can take your coat?" said Wilma with mischief.

"Okay, I am about to do something I've never done before," Suzanne said before another moment passed where nothing happened. "Wilma," Suzanne asked, "How do I know that I'm going to like your body. I mean what if you're all bristly or something."

"Well, do you like it when we kiss? Like this?," said Wilma standing and kissing Suzanne, who murmured a yes. "And what is it that you like about the kisses?"

Suzanne blushed. "You're all soft ... and I like your tongue when you put it in my mouth."

Wilma was so happy that she laughed. "Honey, if you like the kisses, then you'll love the rest."

"Okay," Suzanne said.

"Okay, what?"

"Okay, to make love, but let's go slow. And I want to leave the lights on. If I'm only going to do this once, I want to see everything. ... Do you still want my coat, Ms. ?"

As Suzanne was washing herself, the washcloth and soap cleansing away the sweet thick smells, the sweat, the juices from either cunt, the taste of salt skin, she reminded Wilma, "I have to ask you not to tell anyone. I know it's not fair, but we can't risk what would happen if Julie ever found out." Wilma argued that she should be able to tell Sarine, as long as she promised not to breathe a word. Suzanne thought it peculiar that Wilma would want to tell Sarine, "What if she flips-out with jealousy and goes right to Julie?"

"That," Wilma knew for certain, "is not even a remote possibility. We have a different style of relationship."

Suzanne said wryly, "Oh yah, modern, I forgot." They both laughed.

"And what are you doing in a hotel room on a Friday night with a strange woman, my dear?" Wilma teased.

When it was settled that no one except Sarine would ever know, they went back to kissing. They could hardly get enough, but it was getting onto eleven o'clock, and Suzanne had half an hour to get home before Julie finished her shift. They lingered for as long as they could, and then Suzanne dressed. As Wilma walked her to the door, Suzanne said, "Thank you." Wilma understood. She held the door open for Suzanne and watched her leave.

Wilma didn't want to dress or wash; she threw herself down on the big wrinkled bed where she slept long into the next morning. When she woke, she felt the displacement of waking up alone in an unfamiliar room. She put on her clothes from the day before, checked out and caught a taxi home.

Wilma's composure seemed to be washing off in the shower. She had come home, undressed, put her clothes in the hamper, and turned the shower up full, as hot as she could stand it. She had entered into the hard part, the withdrawal and the letting go. With the water rushing on her, and the sense of loss, she felt herself struggling with dizziness. She wanted to call Suzanne, to talk with her, but she knew that would be breaking their agreement to proceed as if nothing had happened. She finished her shower and, steadying herself, sat down on a chair.

The first few minutes of the opera were starting. Hearing the opera through the door, Wilma realized it was Saturday. Sarine had let herself in and begun their weekly ritual. Wilma was glad to hear her banging pots in the kitchen, sort of singing along.

Wilma gathered herself and entered the big room, where a soprano's voice, filling the rafters, hovered loud in the air. "Thanks for getting everything started, Sarine," Wilma said, her voice sounding shredded and watery. Sarine smiled her greetings, looking up from the steam of the kettles and the heat and the food, but stopped short when she saw how Wilma looked. "What's wrong, baby?" Sarine quickly unplugged the kettle and snapped the dials that turned off the stove and the radio. Silence wafted to the ground, steam dissipated and, like a fire that could no longer conceal itself, Wilma burst into tears.

TURNING THIRTY-ONE

Heather Ramsay

MY FRIENDS HAVE told me, when a woman reaches the age of thirty, there is no turning back. That the big three-o marks the greatest crisis in a woman's life since the first time she tried to insert a tampon and, after five hours of struggle, suddenly realized that she had taped the instruction sheet to the towel rack – upside-down.

Somehow, I always believed it would be different for lesbians. All my friends had their crises and would gleefully remind me that my turn was soon to come. When my birthday finally did arrive, the big event was duly celebrated with a party. The finale of the evening was a snake-dance of dykes, hands on undulating hips that wove between chairs, chip-dip and Chianti, uncoiling amidst hysterical laughter as I symbolically peeled from my flesh a red body-stocking and emerged, a new but older woman, wearing a T-shirt that read: "Oil of Olay Sucks."

Then, I waited patiently for the onset of my first crisis. And I waited – three months passed, soon seven; finally, a year. My older companions gave up on me, and I, why I remained content, blissfully untouched, until the middle of my thirty-first year.

Even now I can recall my day of reckoning. It began on a bright summer Sunday in June. David and I had arranged to go out for brunch; by the time I reached his apartment, my stomach had begun to acknowledge the intrusion of half a cup of coffee and some Crest toothpaste.

I tapped gently, remembering his offhand remark about meeting a friend on Saturday night. No answer. I knocked harder. "The twerp must have a hangover," I thought aloud. Giving up on my reddened knuckles, I tried the doorknob. Luckily, it wasn't locked, and I tiptoed in.

"OK, Fred Astaire," I called as I looked around the living room for signs of life, "it's time to take off your top hat and put on your table napkin." Still no response; I headed directly for the bedroom loudly singing "Good Morning Sunshine." I stepped into cool darkness and the hum of an air conditioner. Kneeling beside the bed, I shook what I hoped was a shoulder hidden under a mound of sheets – it moved. My eyes had not adapted to the darkness; I bent closer whispering sweetly, "David, you stupid faggot, if you don't get up in ten seconds, I am going to leap on that miserable body of yours until. ... "

The sheets edged down slightly, and I found myself within six inches of the bluest pair of eyes I had ever seen.

"No, no leaping," said a very sleepy, but definitely female, voice. "Are you – Jes – Jessie?"

"Yes," I replied, "but you, you are certainly not David!"

She smiled, stretched slowly under the covers, half resting her upper body on her elbows, the sheet discreetly tucked under her arms, and yawned, "What time is it?"

"Noon," I answered sharply. "Here, let me introduce you to the day." I pulled open the curtains, and the sunlight, unfortunately, hit her directly in the face. There was a muffled squawk, and, when I turned, she was again completely covered.

"Oh, my head; my feet; my body," she moaned.

"Pardon. The covers. I didn't quite catch. ... " The front door slammed, but the mound remained silent.

"Jess, where are you? I know I saw your car outside. Have you met Beth yet?"

It was David. I stepped out of the bedroom and leaned against the doorjamb. "Oh, that's her name. So, not meaning to pry, what is she doing here, err, there?" I pointed over my shoulder. "If it wasn't for your wooden-shoe flower pots, I would have thought that I was in the wrong place. As it was, I wondered if the tooth fairy had gone berserk."

"No such luck," he retorted, tossing a carton of Player's onto the couch. "I went to the store in order to consummate my filthy habit. You — you are just too punctual."

"All right, all right," I laughed, "you win. But — let me put it another way — who is she?"

"A friend from work, student summer help. She wanted to see a gay bar, so I took her. Well, we danced 'til dawn or at least until the subway shut down, effectively preventing my friend from returning to her suburban bed. Interested, hmm, a tiny bit?" he said twirling his moustache.

I quickly looked around the room. "Your plants need watering." I felt my cheeks flush. " Let's go eat."

"Can I join you?"

The voice was so unexpected that I started and turned directly into a brown terry-cloth robe. "Excuse me." I backed up, rubbing my nose, trying to refocus the medium-tall brown-haired woman who stood in front of me.

"I'll only be fifteen minutes in the shower."

"That's fine with me." David looked at me. "How about you, Jess? Oh, I almost forgot" — he began to motion with his hands — Beth, this is Jessie; Jessie — Beth."

She held out her hand. "I believe we met, unofficially, a few minutes ago."

"Yes," I smiled, "sorry about the cheap wake-up. He won't pay for the deluxe one. No, no I don't mind either; just hurry."

David handed her a large fluffy blue towel, and she disappeared into the bathroom. Although I had time to vertically appraise this new individual, all I can really remember of that initial meeting is the sensation of melting into those blue eyes.

◆

The afternoon slipped away; I was late. When Mary opened her door, she found me squatting in supplication. I wiggled my bum.

"What are you doing!" She glared down at me, a hand raised in a futile attempt to check strands of hair in mid-flight from under her scarf.

"Begging your forgiveness," I panted, lapped my tongue, and extended a limp wrist. "This is my wet puppy routine. Like it?"

"You are an hour late!" she scowled, turning her back on me.

Both knees cracked as I rose and followed her into the apartment. "Not quite. I have been outside, for at least five minutes, whining and scratching. I thought you would never come."

"What happened? It's not like you to be this late."

"Just falling in lust."

"What!" Her eyebrows rose sharply.

"Oh Mary, stop acting like your virginal namesake. L-U-S-T: lust."

"Have you been drinking?"

"No, but I am high, high on sheer unadulterated lust." I sighed and licked my lips. "I love it."

Mary returned from the kitchen carrying a cup of steaming coffee. "Here, I think you need this. Now, please sit! Your pacing is making me nervous."

I plopped onto the rug. Mary sat down at the table and looked wistfully at her typewriter.

"I know, I know, I promised to help you with your essay. Just let me get this out of my system first."

She crossed her arms, resigned, "OK, get on with it."

"I have spent the entire afternoon salivating into a bowl of ratatouille and longing over a dish of cherry cheesecake, and all because of a child. Well, not exactly a child. I mean, she is twenty-one. Sort of a fledgling adult, wouldn't you say?" Mary didn't, and I continued. "But, compared to thirty-one, I did feel like the elder."

"Is she gay?"

"You always ask the most deflating questions. No, she isn't."

Mary just rolled her eyes. "Don't you think that ten years is a rather large gap?"

"Hold it! I'm not marrying her; I'm only having fun fantasizing. But – hmm – yes, I do confess to feeling somewhat uncomfortable with the age difference. Our life experiences aren't the same. She did hold her own though during our conversation, yet I still felt awkward, guilty even."

"Does 'dirty old woman' strike a chord?" She attempted a leer.

I grinned and nodded, "Perhaps."

Mary leaned against her typewriter, trying to look interested. "So what is she like?"

"Attractive, slender, brown hair, blue eyes," I paused, "a third-year college student, and an aspiring poet. There is, also, a sort of simmering intensity to which I am definitely drawn."

Mary shook her head. "Uh-oh, you're nibbling at the bait."

For a second time that day, I blushed. "I doubt it! But, during the whole time, I did have this lurking sense of 'something' coming from her. Crap! Here I am worrying about attentiveness. I should be flattered. Ouch, the coffee is hot! Besides," I finished my sip, "she's not a lesbian. Becoming attracted to a straight woman is like taking a stroll through Birks – you can admire the merchandise, but can you really afford to take it home with you?"

"I think you've taken the bait all right," she smirked.

"There was one other thing." I sat up and leaned forward. "During dessert, she quite casually mentioned having had a recent affair with a woman friend. It caught me completely by surprise, and I dropped a piece of cake down my shirt." I lightly shook my shoulders. "It still feels sticky. Anyway, when I let her off at the subway, I gave her my number and told her to give me a call sometime."

Mary smiled smugly. "You're hooked."

"Oh shush, let me have my fun. That's all it is — a game, play."

"Just remember," she waggled her finger, "be cool. Now, are you finished? Can we get on with my essay? This one is difficult — a month away, and already I have a headache."

"Right." I moved up to the table. "Where do you want to begin?"

"Here."

"Her name is Beth."

"Jessie!" Mary jabbed the essay outline at me.

♦

Four days passed, and Thursday evening found me at home with a good book. Lack of supper and a glass of wine had almost put me to sleep. ... Ringing! The phone? My mind sluggishly registered the sound of reality as my hand automatically groped for the receiver. "Hello," I mumbled.

"Hi," replied a woman's voice (immediately, I knew), "it's Beth. How are you?"

I could feel my pulse quicken and a tingley warmth move past my knees. "Why Beth," I answered calmly, "it's good to hear from you."

"How did your friend's essay go?" she questioned.

My mind went blank. "Uh? Oh, Mary! Oh fine, just fine, no problems."

"Are you all right?" She sounded concerned. "Did I disturb you?"

Aggh! I was acting like a dewy-eyed adolescent. "No, no, I was only dozing. Hard day at the desk, I guess."

"Well, I was wondering" she hesitated – "if you aren't busy tomorrow," – another pause – "could we have supper together?"

My forehead felt hot. I tried to sound detached. "Unfortunately, I am, but – I have an even better idea." How can I be this bold, I thought? "Come to my apartment for supper on Sunday; I have a new recipe, and I want to experiment, err, try it out."

She laughed. "That does sound like a good idea. What time shall I come?"

"How about five?"

"That's great," she replied.

"Do you have my address?"

"Yes. See you on Sunday. Goodbye, Jessie."

"Bye." The phone clicked, and I was left with the buzz of the dial tone. I hung up and wiped my hands across my thighs and grimaced: oh, the heartbreak of puddle palms. "Supper!!" I shouted, leapt from the couch, and pranced into the kitchen.

♦

Dinner was a success. Not only was the food delicious, but the nervousness that I experienced in my earlier contact with Beth had all but disappeared; I felt relaxed, at ease. After we were settled in the living room, again in conversation, I couldn't help remembering how frivolous my initial attraction had been. The corners of my mouth twitched involuntarily as I thought "She will make a good friend."

"Why are you smiling?" she asked.

"Oh," I replied, "just a passing thought. The food and wine have finally overcome me." I tried to stifle a yawn. "What time is it?"

She looked at her watch. "Oh no, it's almost two; I've missed my train!"

"Do you have the feeling," I rubbed my empty wine glass like a crystal ball, "that this has happened before?"

"Are you being sarcastic?" She sounded offended and her cheeks had turned crimson.

"Only teasing," I said, lightly patting her arm, "only teasing." I sighed heavily. "Frankly, I am too tired to drive you home, so the only other solution, besides walking, is for you to stay here." I ignored the tiny flutter of anxiety in my stomach.

"No, I couldn't. I have to work tomorrow." She stood up quickly. "I'll call a cab."

I hoisted myself from the couch. "Don't be silly; I have to get up too, at six, actually. If you may remember, waking up people is a specialty of mine."

"I'll need to change — "

I interrupted, "What you are wearing now is fine."

"Yes, I suppose you're right." She stared into my eyes. "Are you sure you don't mind, Jessie?" A pause. "I mean, I did only intend to stay for supper."

"Beth," I stared back, "you are welcome to stay. I only ask that you make a decision quickly before I drop at your feet in a coma."

She smiled and shrugged her shoulders. "Since you put it like that, which way is the bedroom?"

"Follow me."

I left her there to get undressed and went back to turn off the lights. When I returned, the room was dark. I stumbled over a pair of shoes and fell onto the bed. Beth was beneath the covers, apparently in a deep sleep — on my side of the bed. I took off my clothes and tried to slide quietly under the sheets, only to begin my regular flailing about until I landed in the right position. She seemed oblivious to all my thrashing. When I finally settled, I began to feel increasingly uncomfortable. Suddenly, I was very much aware of the presence of a warm body only inches away from mine. I resolved that, while distance supposedly makes the heart grow fonder, it also makes it less susceptible to temptation. I turned quickly onto my side and directly into the trunk beside my bed. "Crap!" I gritted my teeth, held my fore-head, and shifted closer and closer to the edge of the bed. I was determined to keep a respectable six inches between her body and mine.

After I hit my head for the fourth time and made my third trip to the bathroom, Beth sat up abruptly and looked out the window.

"Jessie, do you think it's morning yet?" I felt her body turn — "Are you ever restless!"

"Who, me?" I said, biting my pillow case. "Whatever gave you that idea?" I could feel the warmth of her body return as she lay back down. "I thought you were asleep."

The covers moved ever so slightly. "You toss and turn a great deal. Can't you get to sleep?"

"I might have a chance, if certain people would stop talking," I mumbled, pulling the pillow over my head. A hollow "oh" worked its way through the feathers, and I felt her move closer. My territory was being quietly invaded, and I lay immobilized, barely able to breathe. I slowly pushed the pillow away from my face and gently turned to the right, only to have my mouth enveloped by a mass of hair spreading from the head that was now resting on my shoulder. The enemy troops had landed with a direct hit.

"Uh, wha, what are you doing?" I stammered into her hair.

"What do you think?" came the voice from my armpit.

"I'm not quite sure," I replied, trying to push several hairs from my mouth with my tongue.

"I am," she whispered, as she snuggled her body against mine, "cuddling."

"I see," I responded, trying to ignore the fact that my knees had become numb, "do you do this with everybody?"

"No, just with my friends."

"Only the close ones I hope," I muttered sarcastically, noting that everything below my neck was now limp.

"Well," she said as her arm magically crept across my waist, "sometimes it's only being friendly, and sometimes, sometimes it's sexual."

Her words hung in the air while my heart did a Buddy Rich solo. I cleared my throat and concentrated on the ceiling. "I am not sure how you define 'friendly,' but I, I would call this," indicating the length of our bodies with my free left hand, "as, uh, sex-" – my voice went up an octave – "ual."

"Well!" came the exasperated response.

For a second, I weakened and glanced down. I gazed directly into those eyes and was lost, submerged heart and soul, by their blue intensity.

"Kiss me!" It was a demand.

We were both late for work.

◆

Three months later, I was the victim of a heterosexual relapse. Why couldn't I understand that Steven – "Oh, by the way, didn't I tell you, I have a boyfriend; we're practically engaged" – was arriving next week, and she would be too busy to see me. Maybe, if there was time, I could join them for lunch. How would I be introduced, I wondered: as the summer replacement? She replied that there was no need for me to be nasty. After all, it wasn't as if she hadn't taken our affair seriously – it was just that she wasn't gay. If she wasn't a lesbian, I wanted to know, what had we been having every night: pseudo sex? She then said, if I was unable to accept our meeting as a passing phase in her life, that was my problem. I concluded that you are what you eat. This initiated her immediate departure.

"You're not running away from me," I screamed down the hall, "you're running away from yourself!" Beth was not impressed by either my words or my dramatics and disappeared into the elevator without once looking back. The romance was obviously over.

Hell hath no fury like a lesbian scorned. I stomped back to my apartment, muttering obscenities under my breath, and slammed the door. The mirror, hanging on the back, fell to the floor and shattered. I took a deep breath, unsure whether I was shocked more by the loss of love or by the possible gain of seven-years bad luck. Turning away, I threw myself onto the couch and buried my head under a cushion – my rites of mourning had commenced. Some people beat their breasts with style, others do not. I am a sniveler; my face turns red and puffy; my eyelashes curl back; my nose drips profusely; and my sinuses become painfully plugged. After barely ten minutes of hysteria, I was forced to come up for air, two aspirins, and some nasal spray.

As I dragged my body back from the bathroom, I suddenly remembered the poem she had written to me. Like a frenzied Maenad, I found and tore it into shreds. I carried the pieces to the window, pushed out the screen, and prepared myself to enact the definitive statement of our relationship. I flung the pieces into the air and watched in horror as a gust of wind caught and blew most of them right back into the room. Amidst fluttering bits of yellow paper, I crumpled to the floor in tears.

As I entered my second hour of non-stop blubbering, I began to worry. Normally a thirty-minute wailer, this malingering was all wrong. I grudgingly thought ... could this actually be the onset of my long-awaited crisis? Better that than a future of soggy Kleenex I thought, and decided to call someone who would know. ...

"You sound terrible, Jessie. Do you have a cold?" Mary asked.

"No," I sniffed, "I think it's a crisis. Can you come over? I need a dry shoulder."

"Sure," she replied. "Hold tight, I'll be there in twenty minutes."

As soon as Mary arrived, I began to babble about everything, about Beth and myself. When I was at last silent, she gave me a big hug and congratulated me on having passed through the rites of crisis and coming through it as ridiculously as everyone else, including herself, had done. In fact, Mary confessed that her crisis had erupted from winning her local supermarket draw: the prize, a case of Chilean grapes. Outraged, she tried to flush them all down the toilet and destroyed her plumbing.

"Well, now that you have finally blossomed and joined the ranks, I think a celebration is in order," she said, reaching for the phone.

"I'm falling apart, and you want to have a party." I blew my nose.

"Oh come," Mary chided, "look on the bright side. Can you honestly believe that you could have had a future with someone who always sat in the front row of Bryan Adams' concerts?"

"Or who could become engrossed with *The Newlywed Game*," I added. We both laughed. "On second thought, hand me the phone, a party might not be such a bad idea after all."

And it wasn't.

"I Asked About Us"

Daphne Marlatt

Chên / The Arousing (Shock, Thunder)

I WAS WATCHING HER hair flash with the movements of her watching, across from me, across the terry-towelled table, two full glasses of amber between us, the place half empty. Flash back to our entrance: long space of tables, chairs, liquid pool's the floor. A fight? No. It's coming down from the naked boards above our heads. Old rooms, other nights. Watching as she led, shy and decisive, straight to the back corner, women's corner she said all along was there as we circled the block, looking for it.

She was watching for signs, something that pointed the way – like this, familiar, the women present, tougher, sighting along their cues or catching them halfsaid, pool-to-beer-table. Understood. I'm standing in for someone. The only action's two guys, a woman elegant in white shirt, black vest, Indian silver. Stalks their table, colours glistening in the light her shot will break.

It's a good sign. C's eyes move back to engage mine. What is? Smiling – that i could touch it, what is seen in the light her dark eyes shine. Touch wood it holds. The crack of ball on ball and a man's call, Hey Brandy! In the pocket. Give George a break why doncha? Solid.

What is? it's her eyes, the way they turn off sometimes, go
inside, or into seeing something absent. What? she won't repeat
the movement. What is? Oh, everything – evasion or: the
more, i think, than i can see – and then – coming here, drinking
beer together. She's taken three new pennies from the tabletop,
i used these to throw the I Ching this morning (but not *these*?),
three shiney ones (three new wishes). It's the way her past col-
lides inside of how she talks. I want to stay immediate, think
she is.

Hey-George! with the open shirt, who's risen laughing, laughs
at losing, prances like a stonedout pony playing *for* her, "Brandy
loves pool." But she, no eyes for him, is aiming as she rounds
the table cool intensity at us. "Gay people are beautiful." Like
some sign flashing – on whose terms?

C's eyes flash dark to light and dark again, breaking black inside
on the morning. So what did you throw? It's a different question
now. She's throwing, solid. I take out the paper, write "solid."
No, no, laughs deep in her throat, that's not the way you do it.
Oh yes, one line up from bottom, one, and one alone, or maybe
two – and three and –

George's voice comes laughing, Danger view? and Brandy, *Déjà
vu*. Don't you know what that is? What? One hand poised in the
act of throwing – one hand firm on the cue: I've *been* here, man,
been here before.

I watch her throw: to make us present, say we are.

CHEMO DREAMS

J.A. Hamilton

ONLY A MATTER OF hours now, the doctor says.

Only a matter of time dripping away, Amy Browder, oozing; a matter of playing hide-and-seek with death. Ready or not here she comes. Hag real with rotten teeth.

You go in now, Louise. Say your goodbyes.

I look up. Someone remembered me. Why? I don't care why. Amy's sister, swaying gold chains.

Heavy hospital door. Slick smell of cancer wafting. Yellow hotdog breath. Antiseptic. No more tubes or bleeping machines. The family decided. Tick of the hourglass draining. Pulled drapes. No cord of sun, not one.

The light hurts her eyes, the nurse says. Leave them be.

But Amy loves the sun. Eight years we've been together. You don't know. I know everything about her. Please. I just want a minute alone with her. I won't touch the curtains, I promise.

Not her mother, father, brother, sister, husband, child. Not even a cousin. I beg. I have to beg. Just one little minute.

A minute against her eve of silence. How long is a minute, Amy, how much of your sand dribbles out? Amy? Amy? I stroke her pasty forehead, jiggle her shoulder. Wake up wake up now Wake up goddamn you don't die I never thought you'd really die Amy wake up the old crone's got you got bits of you

---

sweating in her hands go after her take brass knuckles don't do this wake up here's Ramona's switchblade I stole it I'll help Please.

Hag humping free and cackling. Jolting cripple walk like water torture, stronger than Amy who used to lift weights, stealing bits of her soul like chunks of bleeding beef in twisted white palms, flesh dangling from dirty six-inch fingernails. Her the vulture, my Amy her feast.

Minute's up.

Amy!

Exiled to the hallway. Better maybe. Collapse in a turquoise visitors' chair a pricked balloon deflating. Amy get out of that hospital bed. I'll take you home baby, tuck you safe and rock you well. Fuck you, Amy. I wish. Fuck your bald head too much chemo chemo chemo wonder what your brain carries now. Chemo dreams sluicing like Mississippi riverboats, baby? We can drink champagne. We can eat artichoke hearts. Only come home honey.

Who's gonna win here, anyway?

Watch out.

Amy is not going to lay down easy.

Look out.

Amy is running hard to catch you, Death, you sly-backed bitch. One hundred-metre dash, four hundred metres, how'd you get away so fast? Amy is tall. She can make time. She had a runner's muscles once. You'll see. Grab your hair coarse as rope, stringy as blue-grey underworld, grab it, ha! spin you, rip your ash robe down the centre of you with one thrust of young fingers. Amy's knuckles are white. Her eyes are glass agates, blue pupils twirling around themselves in a sea of cut emptiness. She will stare you down, cunt. One sloe tit, two. She's ripping shriveled berries from your sunken chest with honed incisors. Sour nipple juice, poison fruit stains Amy's teeth, dribbles black out the corners of her lips across her red lips and out onto her pale chin, under, down her silver gazelle neck while you bleed black from holes in your breasts.

Amy's bone skull shining.

Amy spits your nipples on the dusty ground. She spits on your wail I hear the sound warble, aims clear, shoots well and drowns your hag noise in that arching stream of spittle. Your electric element eyes, circling coils of red-blue fire scorch out, grab Amy's spit like a misbehaving baby's hand hold it tight against them. Steam her phlegm gone. Steal words, fight. Hope?

Whore of life. Amy slams her fist in your face.

Arms fold out.

Who's gonna win here, anyway?

Amy Browder lover cover me mother, be my blanket womb. Moon in your mouth between my thighs. I take your whole fist, hug it hard and come in wedding rings around it.

Tight voice. Tears.

Louise? She's gone.

THE KIDNAPPING

Naomi Binder Wall

I'D LIKE TO TELL a story that no one's ever heard before, about a trip I took a long time ago, before I moved out to B.C.

It was back in the seventies, early on, and I had a bike. So I took off. The bike was big, of course, and I was my usual small self. The first time I stopped to gas up, this burly guy comes up to ask me if I need any help. I hadn't even gotten off the bike yet, so I couldn't imagine how I'd indicated that I might need help.

"Thanks, but no thanks," says I, and I get down off my bike. This guy doesn't work there or anything; he's just the driver of a neighbouring car, waiting to be serviced. He's intrigued by me.

Well, I go about my business, look at a map to decide which way I'm going to travel, and he won't lay off. Am I from these parts, he wants to know. "Nope, just passing through," says I, as I climb on my bike, gear up, and roll out of the service station.

Well, this guy apparently decides he doesn't need servicing, and, before I know it, he's passing me on the sideroad, dust rising like a fog around his car, as he takes off like a bat-out-of-hell for the highway. He's off and gone like a shot.

I ride for about an hour, fairly slowly, when I see this same guy stalled at the side of the road about twelve metres ahead. He's got someone in the car, and his head is under the hood, his emergency flashers flashing, his rear end sticking out, caught like a neon basketball in the glare of the sun. I figure I probably know what's wrong with his car, and, since he's got what looks to me like a woman traveling with him, I figure I'll be safe, so I pull over and ask the guy if he needs any help.

He starts jumping up and down like I've committed some sort of crime. "Are you kidding?" he says. "What are you, some kind of a faggot?" Not one to take this sort of thing lightly, I tell the guy he's an asshole, and that I'm going to offer his girlfriend a ride on my bike, just in case she'd rather travel in polite company instead of with this bigot. He calls me some other sexually deviant name, not believing for a minute that I'm actually intending to offer his girlfriend a lift.

As he sticks his head back under the hood, I stick mine in the open window on the passenger side of the car.

"Hi, you want a lift?" I say to the woman, who looks at me like I'm from Mars. "On what, that motorcycle?" she says. "Why not. It runs a lot better than your boyfriend's car," I answer. Turns out she's already two hours late getting home, her roommate's probably worried sick, and she'd welcome the opportunity to ride on the back of my bike. Of course, she's never done anything of the sort before.

Luckily, I have an extra helmet, which I brought along in case I decided to pick up any hitch-hikers, so I give it to her and pass on a few minimal instructions as to how to sit on the bike, not to lean into the corner, how to hold on, all those things you have to know. Her boyfriend, in the meantime, is mesmerized by the whole scene, and, by the time he gets it together to thwart the kidnapping, we're off, hightailing it up the country highway like two geese returning to the flock. I don't even know her name, or she mine, and I know there's no point starting up a conversation in the wind, so I figure I can wait till we stop for a pee or a bite to eat. All she's bothered to tell me is that she lives about two hundred kilometres straight through.

So there we are, flying along this country road, balmy day, just enough sunshine to keep the chill off. I'm feeling my oats, as they say, and suddenly my friend behind me tells me I have to stop. She sounds kind of urgent, so I slow down and pull over. "What's the problem?" says I. She tells me how she's really uncomfortable and couldn't we stop for a little while. She happens to have a bottle of wine and some cheese in her bag, and I'm feeling hungry, so we stop and chat for an hour or so. She's really interesting, sort of caught between the old and new ways of thinking about women's lot in life. She's not in the least concerned about the whereabouts of her boyfriend, who hasn't shown up or passed us on the road. I'm getting nervous, though, 'cause if he does show up, he might not think kindly of me, an obvious sexual deviant who absconded with his girlfriend.

The next thing I know, the guy shows up, with two Ontario Provincial Police in tow, ranting about how I've kidnapped his girlfriend. I scramble for my driver's license, while my friend, whose name turns out to be Iris, tries in vain to convince the cops that she came along willingly. The boyfriend's jumping up and down, shouting obscenities too vile to repeat, and the two OPP are laughing like a coupla stuck hyenas.

"What's so damn funny?" says the guy. "This girl, or whatever the hell it is, coerced Iris onto the bike and is obviously up to no good. It's your responsibility to do something about it." He is fit to be tied.

Well, the two OPP can't stop chuckling long enough to ask me any questions, so I politely suggest that I'll be on my way, and they can all straighten things out between them without me present.

I've always believed Iris felt sorry to see me go, and I sure felt bad leaving her there. I guess the two OPP wondered how a squirt like me might run off with some guy's girlfriend. I've never forgotten it, though, the fact that I just asked her if she wanted a lift, and she said yes, more or less, and this guy is so freaked out he felt compelled to call in the OPP.

I don't appreciate being the butt of anyone's joke, especially not some jerk like Iris's boyfriend. But if I've gotta keep sticking my neck out – trouble or not – I'll do it. Life's too short to be living someone else's. If just looking at me is enough to set some people off, too fuckin' bad.

Out of Her Skin,
Out of Her Voice

Nila Gupta

Upstairs, my lover, Shirani, and her twelve-year-old sister, Leelaka, are talking it out in Leelaka's bedroom while I sit here in the living room knitting furiously, snapping the wool taut with every knit and pearl. I try to relax, but the more I think about what is happening, the more I pull the wool tighter and tighter.

I want to jump up, unravel myself free, stride up those stairs two steps at a time and tell Leelaka. ... But voices other than my own invade my thoughts, *It's between them ... they have to work it out ... I am not family*, they rebuke me.

Shirani's and Leelaka's voices occasionally descend the flights of stairs. Mostly, I hear Leelaka because she is the more impassioned of the two. She is crying, and the cry is bitter.

I try to breathe deeply and stop all this hmmphing and cheuping that I'm doing. I put down my knitting needles, lean my head back into the deep cushions of their sofa, and close my eyes for a few minutes. Then I get up and search for my knapsack, find my raga tapes, and insert one in their stereo. Playing my raga tapes always calms me. Right now I'm climbing the scales with her and dropping, climbing higher and dropping, climbing higher still and dropping, climbing and dropping, climbing and dropping. She is teasing me, but I'm staying with her rhythm until we finally reach the note we have been striving for. And then I stay with her, there. I stay with her for a long time.

I remember the beautiful, intelligent, curious girl I met a year ago. Leelaka with the ponytail, in Shirani's and Ranu's comfortable hand-me-down clothes that she loved to wear. She showed me her robot routine, her skill in doing handstands and somersaults, and how to breakdance. She would gallop down the stairs in the morning and jump onto the sofa-bed when I used to sleep over, wrap herself in our sheets, lie close to me, whispering her questions about masturbation, periods, and about why she was having yellowish-white discharges. I used to ask her questions about her friends, her school. She was always so glad when Shirani left so that she could talk to me alone. And she would talk on and on.

She was so excited that time we took her to a poetry reading by local women of colour. It would be too late for us to bring her back home so she would have to sleep over at my place. Even though it was only for one night, she wanted to pack a big suitcase! In the morning, I woke up and went and opened the door to my basement apartment to let the light in. I wanted to make it bright and cheerful for her when she woke, but she was already awake though pretending to be asleep. I kissed her forehead. She smiled; she grinned with her eyes closed ... and gave herself away.

The raga tape clicks off, and Leelaka's voice erupts through, interrupting my reminiscing.

"Shirani, you, ... " she sputters so loudly that two flights below I hear her. "You're always talking politics, you're always talking about stuff no one else can relate to. It's always feminism this and lesbianism that, capitalists this and unions that ... and ... imperialists and invasions. ... And all these places in the world I never heard of before – Bhopal, Grenada – god, why don't you just bring in a map and a pointer and pretend you're a teacher. And all this wife assault and rape, and this woman dead and that woman murdered. Every time you come home, you talk and talk about politics, and we can't relate to it, and you expect me to, but you forget I'm only 12, and you expect me to be older, but I'm not, I wish I was, but I'm not. Can't you just talk to me about good stuff – can't we have fun anymore. Why do you have to depress everyone? ... "

That's it! I don't want to hear anymore. I am going to march upstairs and tell that little girl a thing or two about "fun" and "good stuff," and then I am going to tell her about reality. But something in her voice stops me. Chills me to the bone. A weight and assurance behind her voice. Like there are a million people behind her. *You depress everyone.* ... Everyone. Everyone.

My mind is spiraling towards the centre, to the point, to the point I want to understand. I know that Leelaka is only mouthing what her amma and tattha and sister have been saying for a while behind our backs. They want us to keep quiet, keep quiet, keep quiet. But that's not enough for them; they want Shirani to change her life; they want me out of her life. They want her not to be *kush* anymore, not to get involved in politics, not to speak out against lies.

Everyone thinks you're too radical, ... everyone says you've changed. Suddenly, I feel like giving up. There is no arguing with voices like these, that twist everything. Everything that Shirani talks about is politics. We can't even talk about our lives.

Now I'm furious. I never go down without a fight. I want to shout at Leelaka, to shake her to her senses, "Look at you, you've changed! What's happened to you?!"

Now Leelaka's into the preppy style with an attitude to match. Pearls and wool sweaters and make-up and moussed-up hair and dangling earings. Snobbish. Always putting everyone down. Poor people, gay men and lesbians, feminists, her family in Sri Lanka and India; everyone except white rich people because they have "style." If I pointed this out, she would never admit it; she's a liberal. It's always individuals she has problems with, not the group, she insists. But she only talks about individuals she has problems with. And she's become so self-centred too. So critical of Shirani, always finding fault with her, calling her stupid, calling people she doesn't like "gay" despite, *in spite*, that we've explained to her that she's using gay like a swearword and that's offensive. "They're so gay," she says and goes on and on, her mouth screwed up in disgust, until I feel and hear my heart pounding hard and fast in my chest.

♦

My brother and his partner were waiting in the parking lot with their van packed and loaded with all our stuff, ready to go. Shirani's tattha had helped carry some of Shirani's things to the van. He had even wished his eldest daughter well, telling her to call when we got a phone installed.

Shirani's amma was sitting on the couch, in her nightgown, just staring at the door through which we had all been carrying boxes of books, bags of clothes, bricks and planks for her bookshelves, and other what-nots. She had tried to sleep through the whole moving-out process. As Shirani came down the stairs, she averted her face. This had been our final check to see if Shirani had got everything she needed. I said goodbye to Shirani's amma as gently as I could. She didn't respond.

As I walked out the door Shirani said, "Amma, I'm leaving. Aren't you going to say goodbye and wish me well?" I shut the door behind me and didn't hear her response. Five minutes later, Shirani came out of her parent's rented townhouse. Her face was grim. "Amma said that I was welcome to come back any time, but my friends are not to set foot in her house again." That meant me.

I had always been a welcome guest in their home until the day Shirani announced that she was going to be moving into an apartment with me. Her amma had asked Shirani over and over again if I was a lesbian, but she couldn't bring herself to ask if her daughter was one too.

Why can't we all live together? I thought, and then realized that had originally been Shirani's dream. Whenever she used to talk about it, I had always responded with "Well, that's a possibility." But, as I walked with her, I knew I had been lying. I had known it would be impossible. I held her hand as we walked dejectedly towards the van that would carry our belongings to our new home together.

♦

"Shirani, can't we have fun anymore?" Leelaka wails, her voice rolling down the steps.

I send Shirani a telepathic caress, hoping that she can feel it. I want to go up there and say something, to defend Shirani, but I am not supposed to be hearing all of this. So I pick up my knitting needles and head downstairs to the basement to watch some TV. I hate TV, but this is the farthest I can get away from Leelaka. Only dead television voices in all their triviality, lies, and smugness, can shelter me for a while from these real, live, pained ones upstairs.

I wonder if I should go up and ask them to call it quits for now; they've been at it for two hours already. I decide against it. I had never felt Leelaka's resentment against me so acutely as today, and she would certainly not appreciate my "interference."

I walk across the basement floor that now has Leelaka's homework spread out all over it. I plop myself down on the sofa that only last year Shirani and I used to sleep and make love on.

A year of emotional upheavals, I think. A year of Leelaka being used both as bait and ransom by her parents. "Come visit your sister," they would say to Shirani. "She misses you." Come stay the night, the weekend, the week. Come back and live with us. But don't bring *that girl* with you. A year of Leelaka not being allowed to visit us in our new home. A year of Shirani being forced to choose between me or them. "Who are you going to spend the weekend with this time?" And one or the other party angry with whatever she decides.

♦

Earlier this evening, Shirani's parents left for California to celebrate their twenty-fifth anniversary (a present from their daughters – and me, but, I remembered bitterly, that that sweet deed was kept hidden from them). We arrived, tired from work, to greet a sulking child who was not at all glad to be looked after by *us*. All of us had missed dinner, and we were starved. Shirani asked Leelaka what she'd like to eat. Leelaka shrugged her shoulders and kept flipping through the Sears catalogue.

"How about if I make some rice and eggs and heat up the *seeney sambal* and *wattaka* amma made before she left?" Shirani asked.

Leelaka seemed to be absorbed by something in the catalogue and didn't respond, so Shirani had to ask her again what she'd like for dinner. Finally, after many sighs and rustling pages, Leelaka shrugged her shoulders once again and announced to no one in particular, "I don't care." Annoyed, Shirani, wisely took it out on the eggs. Shirani had told me that this type of tension had been going on for the last few months. "Every word I say, everything I do, is wrong in Leelaka's eyes," Shirani had said, exasperated.

I, too, was acutely aware of the tension, but I had convinced myself not to get involved. I reasoned that if I kept my nose in my book of lesbian short stories I wouldn't get myself into trouble.

In this home, with Shirani's parents, grandparents, and other assorted relatives' wedding pictures dominating the room, I found myself getting absorbed in a short story. I found myself hungry and unduly grateful for these lesbian perspectives, even though what I was reading wasn't saying a whole lot about my life, about what affects me as a young Indian woman. I prayed to the *Devi* that one day, one day, I would have more than these shards of broken mirrors to see myself reflected in.

A little while later, I looked up from my book. "The food is ready!" Shirani called me. I joined them at the stove.

They were talking about a woman named Gloria, a friend of Ranu's, whom Shirani and Leelaka met when Ranu brought her over to meet the family.

"Ranu says that Gloria doesn't ever want to come back to our house," Leelaka was saying, as I helped myself to the food. "Why?" Shirani asked, surprised.

Leelaka wrinkled her nose and tossed back her black moussed-up hair before replying, "Because you called her paki."

"Whaat?" Shirani said, shocked. "What are you talking about?"

Leelaka went on, unperturbed, "You know, how you talked about paki this, paki that. ... "

Shirani was so shocked, that she looked like she was about to cry. I reached for her hand to squeeze it. Leelaka continued to talk on about how Shirani called Gloria "paki," about how "pakis smelled." ... We stared at Leelaka in amazement. I could sense Shirani's shock turning to anger.

"Look you," Shirani sputtered, "for your in-for-mation, I did not call anyone 'paki'. ... "

"She's from Pakistan, you insulted her," Leelaka interrupted, hurling this like an accusation. "You embarrassed everyone."

"Look, the conversation was about racism," Shirani said, calming down considerably. "Brown people were, are still, called 'pakis' and in the late sixties and seventies racism was pretty heavy. And it's still heavy; it's just changed form."

Leelaka cheupped, crossed her arms, and stamped her foot impatiently but Shirani plowed on.

"Ever heard of 'paki-bashing'? Shirani continued, now shak-

ing her head. "No. I guess you didn't. You're the new generation. You don't know your roots. You don't know your own
people's history. You don't know that your own people were
getting spat on, beaten up in the streets, in schools, getting
thrown onto subway tracks, attacked in elevators. You were just
a baby. But I remember. I lived through it. Well, they couldn't
beat the knowledge out of us. They wanted us to shut up, keep
quiet. They wanted us to forget that the reason we are here is
because they were there. But they are doing a good job with
you, educating the younger ones, like you, out of your skin, out
of your history, out of your place."

"When Gloria was here, I was talking about how I was called
'paki,' and attacked, and a whole lot more, and this was Gloria's
experiences too, although she may not admit it. Some people
can be so oblivious to their own oppression. ... And who told
you Gloria's not coming back?!!"

"Well," Leelaka uttered with a note of finality, not having
listened to what Shirani had been saying, "she's never coming
here again, and it's because of you." Then in a rush she added,
"You're always talking about stuff no one can relate to. She's
never coming back here. You made Ranu lose a friend." She
turned her back on Shirani and walked away to the living room.
The sudden silence filled the room.

Shirani looked helplessly at me and then said to Leelaka's
receding back, "Don't be stupid. I didn't make Ranu lose a
friend. And you're twisting everything."

"You're the one who's stupid," Leelaka yelled, insulted.

"Shut up, Leelaka," Shirani yelled back, her voice cracking in
frustration.

"Ssshh," I said to Shirani, "don't call her stupid, it doesn't
help."

"Yeah," screamed Leelaka, overhearing, "don't call me stupid, dumbo!"

"Leelaka," I said loudly, "don't aggravate the situation," but before I was finished she was running up the stairs on her spindly legs. Five seconds later we heard her bedroom door slam shut.

"See, see," sputtered Shirani, her arms flailing around in frustration. "See what I have to put up with."

"Yeah, *beti*, I know, I know," I said sympathetically. "Let it cool down for a while."

"Let's go home," Shirani urged. "Let her take care of herself. She doesn't even want us here. I'm not staying here any longer. I'm not going to let her insult me like that."

"*Beti*, we have to stay here and take care of her. You promised your parents. Besides, you're responsible for her. She's only twelve. It's not safe for her to stay alone."

"So what! Let Ranu take care of her."

"Ranu's not the most responsible person in the world. You said yourself that she thinks it's all right to leave a twelve-year-old alone," I reminded her. "You have to take the responsibility."

"No, let's go now," she insisted.

"Shirani," I said, knowing that what I would say would have its desired effect, "just remember for a second, what happened to those young white girls, Christine Jessop, Nicole Morin, and the Black children in Atlanta — they were about Leelaka's age, give or take a few years. What if something happens? What if somebody decides to attack Leelaka? Do you want to carry that on your shoulders for the rest of your life. Your house is so easy to break into, and your neighbours know your parents are away. What if something happens? A week of your time is nothing." By the time I finished my little speech, Shirani had already cooled down considerably, and I felt terrible that I had broken my promise to myself not to get involved. Besides, I wouldn't have minded leaving. After all, Leelaka was Ranu's responsibility too.

"All right, all right. What should I do now? Do you think I should talk to her?" Shirani walked into my arms seeking a hug.

I hugged her tight. "Why is she like this? What's happening?" Shirani said from deep between my breasts.

◆

Shirani and Leelaka join me as I watch TV. I've picked up my knitting again, so I'm not really paying much attention to the show. Leelaka asks me if she can switch the channel. I say "Sure." As Leelaka goes upstairs to find the TV guide, Shirani whispers, in response to my questioning, "We didn't get anywhere, but we agreed to keep talking." I sigh. I'm tired.

"Where's Ranu?" I ask. "It's past 12:00," I note with alarm. "Maybe we should call the restaurant? Shouldn't she be home from her shift already?"

"Yeah, she should be," says Shirani, fingering my knitting. "Hey, you've done a lot of work on this – your scarf's almost finished."

Leelaka comes down the stairs and excitedly tells us that there is a good scarey movie on. She's seen it before, she says, and it's *good*. She switches the channel in a hurry and settles herself down on the sofa to watch. I hate horror movies, but I promise myself I won't watch. I'll just finish my knitting. But I find myself glancing at the screen every time there's a change in the music or whenever a commercial comes on. Eventually, I realize that this is not going to work. I can't protect myself this way. I say to Leelaka, "How about watching something else?" But both of them want to watch this movie.

One scene gets me hooked. A black-haired woman runs to comfort a blonde-haired woman. I'm intrigued. I like watching two women together. I always wonder how they are going to be made to relate to each other. These two are obviously friends. The black-haired woman looks familiar to me. I reason that I've probably seen her in other movies before. I ask Leelaka to tell me what's going on. She tells me that young women are being stalked and killed by a crazy person. "Who's the killer?" I ask.

Leelaka says, "An old woman."

"An old woman?" I laugh. "That figures. Why is she killing other women?" I ask, but I know the answer will be absurd. "What a lie," I say in disgust.

"It's not women who stalk other women, it's men," Shirani says, backing me up. Leelaka has turned her head toward us to say something. And then I remember that we're not supposed to talk "politics."

"It's just a movie," she says.

"Yeah," I can't help replying, "but it's still a lie."

Leelaka has turned back toward the TV and is muttering to herself. I know she's upset again with us for talking "politics." But something deep inside, some ancient knowing, some ancient anger is welling up inside me. I want to turn her around and say to her, "Listen, if it wasn't for our 'politics' we wouldn't be here looking after you. And you need looking after, believe me." But I keep quiet. She's only twelve, a child, a baby, she should be spared the depressing reality. I grind my teeth. She's twelve. Yeah, she's twelve. And I think about how so many children never have childhoods. That childhood is a lie.

If she's old enough to assimilate information then she's old enough to know, old enough to be responsible for what she says and thinks, to be responsible for taking care of her life. But I keep quiet.

I know that she thinks nothing will harm her. I think of all the things that she has against her and find myself echoing silently what my father and mother drummed into my head. Like a broken record, a litany, a chant. *You have three strikes against you. You're brown. You're female. You're not rich. Devi* help you, I pray, like my parents prayed for me. But praying wasn't enough to protect me. Praying won't be enough for her. She has to be given information. She has to know. But I keep quiet.

After a commercial, the music picks up, and I know something bad is going to happen. I try to look away, but I am mesmerized. The black-haired woman goes into the kitchen to get something to drink. She takes a milk carton and pours into a glass. As she raises the glass to her lips, my heart jumps out of my chest. It was blood in the carton!

"Please," I say in a desperate last bid, "Let's watch another movie. I hate horror movies. How can you watch them?!" But no one responds to me. They're both absorbed in the movie. "Where's Ranu," I ask. "Shouldn't she be home by now?"

"Are you getting scared?" Shirani asks, laughing. I'm embarrassed.

"Are they both going to die?" I mutter, peeking through my scarf.

"No, only the blonde-haired one," Leelaka answers matter-of-factly.

"Oh, that's great," I say, miserable behind my scarf, determined not to look again, but Shirani interrupts my struggle.

"Nelum, she looks like you," Shirani says to me, pointing to the black-haired woman. "Remember," Shirani continues, "that picture of you on your parents' balcony when you were younger? How old were you then? Sixteen? She's wearing the same clothes. Look, her jeans and that shirt, and her hair is parted in the middle and black like yours. Except, she's white, of course."

I look at the TV screen through my scarf and recognize the black-haired woman. What am I doing in a horror flick? I think, for a moment confused. The black-haired woman says she is going to the bedroom to shut and lock the windows. The music is building up again.

"These movies are made just to terrorize women," I mutter. But then I remember I'm supposed to keep quiet about these things. I glance over at Leelaka. And suddenly I want to shake her.

The music is building up again. My stomach feels even more queasy. My heart is racing again. On the TV screen, the black-haired woman is about to open the door. *Don't do it*, I want to warn her. *Don't open the door.* The blonde-haired woman is sitting in the other room, catatonic. *Help your friend*, I want to scream at her. I want to shake her awake, aware, and ready to fight. Don't let her do it alone, but now I'm despairing, my heart is sinking. The music jumps. I want to scream, to warn her, but I keep quiet.

Now the black-haired woman is opening the bedroom door. Somewhere upstairs, I think, a door slams. "Is that Ranu?" I want to ask, but my eyes are riveted on the black-haired woman. Her hand on the bedroom doorknob is small, like mine. I can almost feel the coolness of the brass knob under her hands; how cool it must feel under her hot sweaty palms. Something is welling up inside me, rising. The door creaks open: the music is like a heart beat, now racing, racing. Then, the door opens to reveal a shadow with a knife, shining, upraised. ... I close my eyes tight.

A woman's screaming fills the room, so loud, all around me, all around me. She is screaming, screaming, screaming. Other voices fill the room. I open my eyes. Shirani and Leelaka are yelling at me to "shut up."

I'm shocked. I'm hurt. Tears are stinging my eyes. Shirani *never* shouts at me, she *never* says "shut up" to me.

◆

No one seems to be breathing in this room. Then Shirani turns to Leelaka. "Turn off the TV," she says quietly.

I know that I am going to cry if I stay here a minute longer. Feeling lightheaded and dizzy, I head up the stairs, telling them I'm going to the bathroom. I know that as soon as they get home, Leelaka will tell her parents I'm crazy − that I was screaming out of control, all because of a movie. But I don't care. I can't keep quiet − I can't be kept out of my voice any longer.

CONTRIBUTORS' NOTES

MARY LOUISE ADAMS is a writer / editor on the editorial board of *Rites* magazine and is a co-editor of *Resources for Feminist Research / Documentation sur la Recherche Féministe*.

CAROL ALLEN was briefly involved with the Lesbian Writing and Publishing Collective but had to leave due to the pressures of being a full-time student at the University of Toronto. She is actively involved in lesbian-feminist politics and is currently working with Lesbians of Colour, and the International Women's Day Planning Committee in Toronto.

BEATRICE BAILY, Jamaican-born, received her Bachelor of Fine Art from York University, Toronto, in 1981, specializing in sculpture, printmaking and painting. Over the last five years Bea has participated in numerous group exhibits. Most recently she participated in Black Perspective Art History and Gallery 940's Black Women group show.

ANNE CAMERON was born August 20, 1938 in Nanimo, B.C., Vancouver Island. "Leo with Leo rising (stubborn as hell), mother of two sons, two daughters and a large pack of 'extendeds.' I've lived on seven acres of rain forest for the past five years with my Sweetie. I have more than fifty rabbits, twenty wild turkeys, four ducks and an ever extrapolating flock of wild chickens." Publications include *Dreamspeaker*, *Daughters of Copper Woman*, *The Journey*, Earth Witch, *The Annie Poems*, and *The Weeping Woman*.

MAUREEN FITZGERALD used to work as an anthropologist / academic and now works as an editor / teacher. She is a co-editor of *Still Ain't Satisfied: Canadian Feminism Today* and is presently working on a history of lesbians in Toronto with the Lesbians Making History collective.

JANINE FULLER is a feminist performance artist who lives in Toronto but will perform anywhere.

CANDIS J. GRAHAM lives in a small, crowded Ottawa apartment with her companion, Wendy Clouthier, and their new computer. Her short fiction has appeared in *Women and Words: The Anthology / Les Femmes et les Mots: Une Anthologie*, *Noovo Masheen 3*, and *Fireweed*. She also writes essays and book reviews. She supports herself by working part-time as a bookkeeper. "Aprons and Homemade Bread" is dedicated to the poet, Joan Bridget.

NILA GUPTA is a First World kush (lesbian) feminist. She immigrated to Canada with her family when she was six years old and is now living in Toronto. This is one of her first stories to be published. Her dream deferred is to be a filmmaker.

J. A. HAMILTON is a Vancouver writer.

KATE LAZIER is originally from Nova Scotia and has lived in Toronto for the last four years. She is involved in feminist and gay publishing, is a part-time student and circulation manager, and a sometime writer.

DAPHNE MARLATT was born in 1942 in Melbourne, Australia. She spent her early childhood in Penang, Malaysia, and immigrated to Vancouver with her family in 1951. Known primarily as a poet (*Steveston*, *What Matters*, *How Hug a Stone*, *Touch to my Tongue*), she has also published a prose narrative, *Zocalo*, and has recently completed a novel. Talonbooks published her selected writing, *Net Work*, in 1980.

She has co-edited several little magazines and is a founding member of the feminist editorial collective TESSERA which publishes Québecoise and English-Canadian feminist criticism and theory. Most recently, two bilingual chapbooks of "transformed" poetry, written and translated in collaboration with Nicole Brossard under the titles *Mauve* and *character*, have appeared with La nouvelle barre du jour and Writing presses.

JENNIFER LEE MARTIN "I am aware of the political and personal reasoning behind some women's choice to call themselves dykes but I don't agree with that reasoning. I think that we should, as women and as lesbians, define ourselves but I don't agree that we can change the power of a word and, more to the point, I do not choose to define myself as a dyke. Words are powerful tools and I don't believe that we can change their value by simply deciding that when *we* say dyke it will have a positive connotation but when *they* say dyke it will have a negative one. When I hear dyke I don't hear love, I don't hear strength, I hear the men yell it at me on the streets, I hear accusation, I hear bigots, I hear danger. I'm not a magician, I can't make the word sound positive, I can't do anything with it but reject it. In rejecting it I also reject the reality that it claims to represent, the image of lesbians that I was taught as I grew up; part of my definition of myself rests on that rejection. I am not a dyke."

INGRID MACDONALD is a writer and visual artist. She is a member of the collective of *Broadside*, a feminist newspaper in Toronto.

DIANA MEREDITH is rediscovering her artist past. Ten years ago she was a sculptor and potter but was side-tracked from the arts by earning a living and coming out as a lesbian. Recently she started performing and writing in the context of the women's community and its issues. Her one-act play *Marilyn Monroe and the Snow Queen* was part of a Toronto conference on pornography and prostitution. She is currently working on a performance piece about Superman and Barbie Dolls.

SUNITI NAMJOSHI was born in 1941 in Bombay, India. Her books include *From the Bedside Book of Nightmares*, *Feminist Fables*, and *The Conversations of Cow*. At present she teaches at Scarborough College, University of Toronto.

ORIENTAL-ASIAN COYOTE doesn't consider herself a writer but the idea excites her. This is her first writing piece. She feels she lives much too far away from the "centre" of Toronto's dyke community.

MICHELE PAULSE was born and lived in South Africa long enough to know and remember. She has been living in North America longer than she likes to admit. She moved from Vancouver to Toronto three years ago wanting to face new challenges; writing is just one of them.

ELLEN QUIGLEY is a poet, a critic and an editor. She is doing her best to convince the Women's Press that the publication of poetry is a worthwhile cause. She is co-editor of *Canadian Writers and Their Works*, a twenty-volume series of critical essays, and has had poetry and criticism published in a number of Canadian journals.

JUDITH QUINLAN is a writer and physiotherapist living in 100 Mile House, B.C. She is presently working on setting up a women's centre in 100 Mile House and developing Zone Three – a women's conference centre and retreat. She spends the rest of her time learning how to survive and grow outside the urban feminist ghettoes.

HEATHER RAMSAY "As a member of the editorial collective, I would like to express my personal dissent with the way in which the issue of racism is discussed in our *Notes About Racism in the Process*. In terms of our collective experience dealing with racism within the context of producing this anthology, I believe we should have and could have presented a deeper and more innovative analysis of our collective process as it related to racism and to lesbian writing in general. Some of this particularly could have addressed responsibility without power and how and why we continued to work together. However, I do respect the position of the collective in that at this point in our development, the other members felt unable to meet my need for discussion."

NORA D. RANDALL is a lesbian feminist living in Vancouver, B.C. She writes for TV, radio, the stage, magazines and newspapers. She has driven an egg truck, a fish truck, rush delivery, taxi and school bus.

JEAN ROBERTA "I was born in California in 1951 and spent my childhood in southern Idaho. In 1967, I moved to Saskatchewan with my family and became a Canadian citizen in 1974. In my last year in high school, I was the Saskatchewan winner in the Canada Permanent Trust Annual Student Writing Contest; I have won several other prizes in writing contests since then. I have taught English and do much unpaid journalistic writing for magazines and newsletters. I have had several poems and short stories published in anthologies.

"I have a daughter, born in 1977; we are an international and multiracial conglomerate. I disapprove of oppression, poverty, war, etc., and have joined groups against them all."

SARAH SHEARD lives and works in Toronto. Her fiction has appeared in the usual Canadian literary magazines. Her first novel, *Almost Japanese*, published in 1985, has been accepted for forthcoming American and U.K. publication. She is currently working on another novel.

NAOMI BINDER WALL, a Jewish lesbian, is a political activist in Toronto. She has a daughter, fourteen, and a son, twenty. A teacher of English as a Second Language, she has written numerous articles on education and women's issues, a bibliography of non-racist, non-sexist children's books for classroom use, is active in the Central America solidarity network and works with the Regent Park and Area Sole-Support Mother's Group. "The Kidnapping" is dedicated to the memory of her great and good friend Pat Smith.

MARLENE WILDEMAN was born 1948 in Lacombe, Alberta, brought up on British Columbia sawmill and dairy-farm culture, and now lives in Montreal where she works as a bilingual medical secretary, translator, reviewer and proofreader. She is currently preparing a collection of her short fiction and translating Nicole Brossard's collected lesbian-feminist literary theory and prose, *La Lettre aérienne*.